Choosing me

Book I

D S Johnson – Mills

Choosing Me

Woodbridge Publishers

1200 Century Way, Thorpe Park,
Leeds, LS158ZA

Copyright © 2023 D S Johnson - Mills
All rights reserved.

First Edition

ISBN (Paperback): 978-1-916849-15-0

ISBN (Hardback): 978-1-916849-16-7

This novel is entirely a work of fiction. The names, characters and incidents portrayed in it are the work of the author's own imagination. Any resemblance to actual persons, living or dead, locations or events is purely coincidental. No part of this publication may be reproduced, stored in retrieval system, copied in any form or by any means, electronic, mechanical, photocopying, recording or otherwise transmitted without written permission from the publisher. You must not circulate this book in any format.

If applicable
Cover Design by Woodbridge Publishers.

Acknowledgements

Firstly, I would like to thank my sister for telling me I had something special.

My oldest girlfriend, Bobb, I will always appreciate your honesty.

I would also like to thank the numerous editing and publishing companies who worked on my manuscript, namely The Word Tank, Fiction Feedback, and Woodbridge Publishers.

Lastly, to my husband, thank you for being my first marketing guru and providing copious amounts of lemon and ginger tea.

Choosing Me

For my Grams, Jane.

D S Johnson - Mills

Table of Contents

Prologue...1

Markus..24

Complication 53

Impulsive 82

Proposition 98

The First Cut 117

Falling in Deep 133

Happy 160

Selfless 183

Mood Swings 214

Revelations..247

Balancing 282

Canary Place 305

Birthday Surprise 331

The Ugly Truth 354

Choosing Me

Dylan's Choice

I love them dearly, I do,
But leaving them was my first clue,
The instant that I became free,
Was the moment I decided to choose me.

Prologue

May 1996 – Plymouth, Mass

The fireworks illuminate the dusky glow of the early evening sky. The noise is welcoming as it drowns out the shouting in my head. I thought coming home would make it better, but instead, it's louder.

The upbeat sounds of sweet home Alabama blare over the boom box as Kizzy grabs our Grams' hands. They start to dance, singing at the top of their voices. Both are laughing joyfully, but the image is making me sad. It was Papa Kit's favourite song. Every fourth of

Choosing Me

July, he would play this record, and they would dance together.

They are beautiful, swaying in unison, my sister, and my grandmother.

Kizzy's youthful glow, her seventeen-year-old nubile body clad in a white bikini top and short jeans, her legs long and lean, contrasted majestically with our grandmother's timelessness. Her silver hair has turned golden in the fading sunlight.

"Do you want to dance?"

I turn to Sam's voice; his hand is outstretched. He used to be my dancing partner, but that was back when he and I were just friends. I smile and take his hand, and his face lights up with a huge smile.

I glance over his shoulder at the girl he came to the party with because she's staring at us. I recognise her vaguely but cannot recall her name. We dance, but when the song ends, I pull away and walk inside the house, not bothering to look back.

Alone in my bedroom, with the door closed, I sit on my bed and cry. The sobs wrack my entire body, but no sounds escape. I don't know why I'm crying, I don't know why I'm sad, but I know I've felt like this for most of my nineteen years.

"Dilly? Are you in here?"

I must have fallen asleep. The light goes on, and my sister's eyes open wide.

"What the hell's going on?"

I rub my eyes, feeling oddly lighter after my nap,

"What do you mean?"

"You're sleeping in the middle of a party?"

"Kizzy, I'm tired."

"No. You're moping over Sam, but I don't know why. Just take him back. He wants to be with you."

"In case you hadn't noticed, he came here with someone else."

"Not really," she says softly, looking down at her feet.

"What does that mean?" I glare at her.

It is so like her to meddle in my affairs. I know

she means well, but honestly, this Sam thing is going to be an ongoing saga between her and daddy.

"I told him to bring a date. I thought it would make you jealous, and then you two would..." she starts, but I cut her off.

"Sam and I are not engaged anymore. He is free to be with whoever he chooses. We are not going to work anything out because there is nothing to work out, so stay out of it."

I stand too quickly, and my neck muscles click painfully,

"Ouch," I say, "Is the party over? I'll help with the clean-up."

"Yes. Grams got tired and went to bed. Sam came back to help tidy up," she says.

"I think he wants to talk to you," she adds, making me snap.

"There's nothing to say, please. I just want some peace."

"Dilly, he's upset, and you're hurting. You've been so

down since you got back from college. Grams and I threw the party to cheer you up."

This softens my resolve. I love these two women with all my heart.

"Sam slept with another girl," I say.

Kizzy's reaction is instant. She flies out the door and down the stairs, making quite a racket. I look at my watch; It's almost one in the morning. She's going to wake Grams, and then there'll be hell to pay, so I groan and run after her.

"You cheated on my sister?"

Sam is in the kitchen, wearing yellow gloves, washing the glass stand that the cupcakes were on earlier. He looks over at me as if in shock.

I told him I wasn't upset and meant it, but telling Kizzy was the only way to stop her from working overtime.

"Yes," he says, nodding his head, his eyes never leaving mine.

"How dare you? Get the hell out, Samuel

Anthony, and don't bother coming over anymore," Kizzy's voice is like steel.

Sam begins to cry, and I remember my own tears from earlier. There was no one to hear or see, so I had no comfort, but I go to him. It really isn't his fault. I agreed to marry him on a whim because it made my family happy. I created this mess and hurt someone I genuinely care about. My head was ready to do it, but my body did not cooperate.

"Save the crocodile tears for your side piece," Kizzy says rather nastily.

"You mess with my sister, and I go for the jugular," she says.

It takes me several hours to calm him down while sitting in his car outside our house. He wants to kiss, and I let him. He fondles my breasts through my thin t-shirt, pushes my bikini top to the side, and caresses my bare legs. I'm pretty sure that I should be aroused, but I'm not.

He soon gives up, and terror causes my body to go rigid. I want to do it with him because I know that he loves me, but I don't move a muscle. I allow fear to wash over me, as it's a feeling I'm familiar with, but sexual desire is unchartered territory.

We fall asleep in his car, holding hands. The early morning rays of the sun, shining into the window of his Mustang, wake me. I stir and open my eyes, and he is looking at me.

"I love you," he says.

"I know," I reply. It's all I have right now.

I watch from the pavement as he drives away, then walk to the back of the house, strip down to my bikini, and wade into the cool salty water. The beach is deserted at this time in the morning.

There are no remnants of the party last night. I swim until my limbs are heavy with fatigue, delighting in the gentle push and pull of the waves. It's still quite early when I enter the house to shower and dress for the day ahead.

Kizzy is fast asleep. It's her weekend off. I'm in the kitchen starting breakfast when Grams appears, greeting me. She has a peculiar look on her face, and my heart sinks.

"Grams, sorry for sleeping out in the car with Sam."

Our grandmother has a strict rule about boys being at the house past nine in the evening. She continues to stare at me, and my heart flips over, wondering if she's mad.

"Nothing happened," I say.

"Why not, Dilly?"

This question throws me, and I am not sure how to respond.

"Is there tea?" she asks.

I make up her teapot and bring it over to her, placing it to the side and pouring her a cup.

"Dilly, sit down. I want to talk to you."

I pull out the chair slowly and sit.

She pours some of the tea into my mug. The spicy ginger smell invades my nostrils. I don't look at her as I'm ashamed that she might think I'd had sex in the car with Sam.

"You don't love Samuel."

It's not a question. I shake my head no, and she gives me the "look," one that says to open my mouth instead of nodding my head.

"No, I don't love Sam."

Grams sighs heavily, shaking her head.

"Rosemary Johnson, you've lived a thousand sunsets, and yet you never learn," she says, sipping her tea.

"When you accepted his proposal, I had a notion something was wrong. You weren't giddy, but I told myself that Dilly is not a giddy type of girl. She is serious and studious, but that's a load of tosh. Every girl in love is giddy."

"Everyone was so happy for us. I thought it would come later," I admit.

"What would come later?"

"I'd fall in love with him. You always said that you didn't love Papa at first but that he loved you. I know Sam loves me so...," my voice trails off.

Choosing Me

"When Kit asked me to marry him, I said yes, but I did not love him. I was in love with another boy. His name was Pagan Jefferson the Third, he was visiting his great aunt over in Braintree, and he was exciting and extremely hot."

I laugh out loud, and Grams smiles, "I was once young too."

"I don't have to tell you the rest of it. Thank heavens I didn't get myself with a child. Anyway, you can imagine how I felt when he left. The only smart move I made was when he asked me to marry him; I said no. I didn't want to break my promise to Kit."

"What did you do?"

"I told your grandfather a week before the wedding. Naturally, he was upset and left the house. I thought that was it. I waited for days in agony, thinking he would call off the wedding and tell everyone what I did. The thing that surprised me the most was I wanted to marry Kit. I knew he was going to be reliable."

We've heard this story many times, but this is the

altered version. She always said it was a dose of cold feet. Not that she had been carrying on with another man behind his back.

Obviously, I know how it ended. They got married and loved each other until death.

"What are you saying, Grams, that I should marry Sam?"

"No, I want my granddaughter to listen to her heart. It won't steer you wrong."

"Sometimes my heart hurts, and I don't know why. I don't feel anything for anyone apart from you, daddy, and Kizzy."

She appears shocked at my words. Her hand trembles as she drinks her tea, and I sip mine slowly.

"What about Lily?"

With those three words, my air supply is restricted, it's as if my chest has been ripped open wide, and I start to cry. Finally, the sobs break free, and they are loud. Grams takes my hand and sits me on her lap. I try to move away, worried I might crush

Choosing Me

her, but she holds me like she did when I was five years old.

My crying wakes Kizzy, and she comes running down the stairs. She rubs my back soothingly. I can hear her telling Grams what Sam did. Kizzy calls him a two-timing bastard.

Grams doesn't tell her to watch her mouth. She doesn't tell me to save my tears for a dry spell like she always does. She lets me cry, and when I am spent, exhausted beyond belief, I fall asleep sitting on her lap with her arms around me.

* * *

The fading sunlight on the blue shutters indicates the sun is about to go down. I lay back on my hands, pushing my freshly manicured toes into the soft wet sand. I am so deep in thought that I don't hear when Grams approaches.

I had taken her into town in Papa Kit's truck to run some errands earlier. She was acting a little secretive, and I wondered what she was up to. Something tells me that I am about to find out.

Since my meltdown a few days ago – which I am a little embarrassed about – both Grams and Kizzy have been acting very cautiously around me, as if they are afraid that I will start with the waterworks again. Work is also a little awkward since everyone knows now that Sam and I are no longer an item.

What can I say? Sexual dysfunction? Triggered by what? Abandoned child syndrome? Kizzy seems to manage just fine.

I sigh.

"It sounds like you have the weight of the world on your shoulders," Grams says.

I shield my face from the glaring rays.

"Sorry, Grams. I don't mean to be moping."

"And yet, here you are," she says, "Come inside. I want to show you something."

I follow her up the pathway leading to the picket fence separating the house from the beach, dusting my shorts with my hands. I stop at the water pump to rinse the rest of the sand from my toes before going inside and sliding the door shut.

Grams is already sitting in the spacious dining room. On the table in front of her is a large binder. She removes a white envelope with a window and passes it over to me. I open it tentatively.

Inside is an airline ticket.

"What's this?" I ask, suddenly excited, "Are you going on a trip?"

Grams has always told us that it was her dream to travel the world once she and Papa Kit retired. But it never happened. Instead, they had to take care of their grandchildren. It must have been hard for them, having lost their only daughter to an unknown enemy.

"Have a look at the ticket, Dilly."

It is made out in my name.

"London?" I whisper, "Grams, I can't go to London. I have work, and daddy wants to take us to Key West, and Kizzy is looking forward to going..."

My voice trails off as she gives me a look I don't recognise.

"Dilly, you are depressed."

"No, Grams. Not really. It's the course. I never should've taken psychology, but next year I'll change my major to finance. I've already decided I'm going to talk to daddy. I can just attend U Mass next fall and live at home. I don't like Yale."

"I think a change of scenery will be good for you."

"But London is so far. Can I not just go to New York instead?" my voice is softer when I say this, and she gives me a sharp look.

"To be closer to Lily? Your sister will spit nails, and I am too old to put her over my knee, and we both know Brandon will not touch his precious Kizzy."

My eyes drift towards the window. The sunlight has disappeared, and a dusky light remains, turning the white sand blue. Grams reaches out her hand to caress my fingers. Her palm is warm and papery.

"Brandon loves you, Dilly."

"I know."

Choosing Me

"I think with you, it's harder because you look so like Lily, but you are not her, and as long as I have breath in my body, you will not end up like your mother. I want you to live; Be happy."

"I could never be happy without my family around me."

"We are here now, and you are not happy."

"It doesn't mean I want to go away by myself. Grams, at least come with me."

"Dilly, part of growing up is knowing when to let go and travel the rough roads by yourself. If you can do that, then you can do anything. But first, you must know when to choose the most precious thing. What do you think that is?"

"Me, I have to learn to put myself first."

* * *

"London?"

Kizzy's face registers her shock, "When?"

"Fourth of July."

"I thought we were going to Key West?"

She is sitting next to daddy and turns to look at him. They are both facing across from me. He is yet to utter any words.

"Daddy, say no. Dilly can't go halfway around the world for an entire month on her own."

I want to point out the obvious, but it won't work with my sister. She will only find another angle to argue. I'm nineteen, so I am legally free to go wherever I choose without parental consent. Daddy cannot stop me, but I would still like his approval. It is hard to admit that sometimes my own father cannot bear to look me in the eye.

"The boys and I played in London once. Victoria Park, in the East end. It was a summer Soca rave," he says.

"Really, daddy? You never said."

"It was a long time ago," he replies, "Do you have a place to stay?"

"I do. Grams and I have arranged everything. I'm staying at the Park View Hotel. It's quite close to Trafalgar Square."

Choosing Me

Kizzy shoots daggers at me, and I glare at her. This is low, even for her. The waiter comes to take our order. Dinner at the Eastbay grille has been a firm staple in our calendar ever since Kizzy and I were little girls. According to daddy, they make the best steak in town. I like it because of the laid-back ambience and the view. With the tall glass windows, I always have the sensation that I am out in the middle of the ocean.

We all order the same thing, but Kizzy tells daddy that he should order a baked potato instead of fries, and he relents. A pang of something akin to jealousy stabs through my heart. It is always so easy with Kizzy and daddy. She only has to command, and it will be granted. It is not long before she returns to the matter at hand.

My eyes wander outside at the view. The seagulls are perched on a bleached piece of driftwood out in the ocean. I listen to my sister as she makes her argument to our father of all the many reasons why I should not be allowed to go travelling on my own. She mentions the recent bombings in London.

Daddy is distracted when Ned, the owner of the

restaurant, comes inside the door with his two teenage sons. Their eyes zone in on us, and they come over to say hello. When they ask about our plans for the summer, daddy surprises me.

"Dilly is going to London," he says.

Ned is impressed with this bit of information. Gushing about how much he loves London. He grabs a biro and writes down the name of the best food markets to visit. I place the paper with his suggestions in my purse. Not even Kizzy's sulking face can stem my excitement. Our food arrives, and we say goodbye to Ned. His eldest son Jared is giving Kizzy the side eye, and I am tempted to point it out just to annoy her. She detests him.

"Kizzy, since Dilly is going to London, I was thinking you could invite Carrick to come with us to Key West."

Kizzy's eyes widen, and her mouth falls open at the same time. It is almost comical, but I don't laugh. I stare at our father. Sam is the only boy that he can tolerate. He never likes any of Kizzy's boyfriends.

Choosing Me

"Really, daddy?"

"Yes, If Dr and Mr Greene are okay with it. Separate rooms, of course," he adds, watching as she pours red sauce on the side of his plate.

"Yes, of course, daddy," she replies innocently.

She replaces the lid of the sauce before reaching over to kiss his cheek, and then she turns to me.

"Dilly, I'll help you pack."

When I look over at daddy, he is cutting into his steak.

* * *

True to her word, Kizzy goes overboard. Not only does she pack my suitcases and carry-on pack, but she also styles my hair in tiny micro braids that take hours, but the result is spectacular. My naturally curly tresses fall bone straight down my back. She and Grams spend ages picking out my outfits, and daddy brings me travellers' cheques and a master card to use only in an emergency, so I have more money than I will need.

It's the night before I fly out, and Kizzy and I are sitting on the floor in my bedroom. Our neighbours have started early celebrations for the fourth of July, and the sharp fizz of fireworks slices through the air. Kizzy crawls over to the window, prying it open, and the noise filters into the room — the sounds of freedom. I am super excited about my trip.

"Dilly, can you bring George Michael back with you?"

"Definitely, Kiz, but only if you promise to share."

She sighs dreamily. It is the one thing my sister and I have always agreed on; we love George.

"I call dibs on all his evenings," she says.

"That's fine. He can sing to me all day long."

"Dilly, you're the best."

She leans her head and shoulders further out of the window. Her long dark glossy hair floats in the gentle breeze, stirring up by the waves coming off the ocean. I crawl over next to her and do the same.

The acrid smell of smoke is strong as colourful

fire lights up the sky. The heat from the day lingers. Way out in the distance, the flashing beam of the Harbour Inn Lighthouse grants the ships gliding over the black ocean a safe passing.

"Hey, Kizzy. Can you do me a favour?"

"Sure."

"Don't be mad at Sam."

She gives me a sharp look, shaking her head.

"It wasn't his fault."

"Did it just jump out and run off without him knowing?"

I laugh at the image she conjures, then sigh. She rubs my back, and I almost purr from the pleasure.

"There's plenty of fish in the sea, Dilly."

I sit on the floor, and she moves next to me. I tell her what happened, and she is quiet for some time.

"I think there's something wrong with me."

"No, you're just overthinking it, and Sam was way too intense. It's a big turn-off when boys start talking about love and marriage, so I'm not surprised."

"Don't you love Carrick?"

"No. It's just fun, a lot of fun, but we're off to college next year, so this is not long-term. Which reminds me."

She crawls over to the opened suitcase spread out on the floor at the entrance to my closet. She pulls out my toiletry bag, unzips it, and holds up a packet of condoms. I groan.

"A girl can never be too careful."

"Kizzy, put that away. Grams will see."

"You just need to let your hair down, Dilly. Men are so easy, and they constantly fall at your feet, so trust your instincts, stand back, and watch them form a line."

Choosing Me

Markus

March 2000 - London

He leads me into the nightclub. I imagine dark and grungy walls stained with unspeakable acts of lust and fear. I really shouldn't be here, but I'm with Toby, my best friend. The men and women stare openly at him, not that I blame them. With his olive skin tone and chocolate brown eyes, he is easily the most beautiful man in the town tonight. He is sixfeet tall with lean muscles, the picture of a modern-day Adonis.

He brings excitement to my otherwise dull and lacklustre existence.

He could lead me down the paths of hell, and I would follow. This is what loneliness does to a good girl.

I think of our meeting in a divisible way. My life has changed after meeting Toby. It must drive Kizzy mad when I speak in this way. I laugh out loud, and Toby turns to look at me but does not react; evidence that he is used to me. We were made for each other, and I cherish the day we met — my wonderful year of magic.

I was on my way to lunch at the firm where we both work when I first laid eyes on him. He was walking down the hallway toward me. I smiled and said hello. The rest is history. He told me later that he knew I was the real deal as I had such a genuine smile.

Toby doesn't appear to have a lot of friends, even at work. He is the head of his department and is always cool and professional, but once he removes that tie, he lets his hair down, figuratively speaking, of

Choosing Me

course.

Toby is bald, but he pulls it off effortlessly.

Tonight, we are at a gay club. Toby never advertises his sexuality, which intrigues me.

He tells me he has invited a friend. They will have drinks and catch up while I dance the night away.

That is the plan, but when Toby and I are out in the town together, things don't usually go to plan.

I'm curious about his friend. I wonder if they are lovers, but when I question Toby, he laughs but does not deny or confirm my suspicions.

The interior is spacious inside the club, with tan leather seats, exposed brick walls, and a huge, glittering disco ball. There's not a dirty glass in sight. I finally begin to relax.

I immediately spot the "friend" because he's looking in my direction. He has an intense kind of stare. Toby walks toward him.

"Markus!"

"Toby!"

They embrace warmly. I slowly approach.

"This is my mate from school, Markus Mills. Markus, this is my girl, D."

"Hello, Dee."

I notice his startling green eyes, stunning.

"Finally, I meet someone besides Gina who actually knows Toby from back in the day. So, I guess my theory of the man from Mars is null and void."

"I don't know. He did appear out of the blue to challenge me and knock me off my podium,"

Markus speaks in warm clipped tones.

"He still has that annoying quality."

"Where did you find her?" Markus asks Toby.

"I don't know her. She's been following me around all night. I've been trying to shake her, but it's tougher than I thought."

Toby tries to disown me. He does this occasionally. Head held high, I walk away from them and hear their laughter. I saunter over to the bar and sit on a stool, spinning around to face them.

Choosing Me

As they approach, Markus' eyes travel up my legs. My already too-short leather miniskirt hikes up when I sit down. My heart skips a beat as his eyes meet mine.

"What would you like to drink?" he asks.

"Water on the rocks with a hint of lemon!" Toby replies.

I chuckle along with Toby. Markus continues to stare at me, and suddenly, the joke is not so funny anymore.

I wonder why he stares so openly.

The bartender comes over, and Markus orders a non-alcoholic cocktail.

"I don't drink alcohol," I explain, "That's why Toby is making fun of me."

I spin around to face the bar, but I sense Markus still looking at me.

"Never?" he asks softly.

"No, not at all. But you're not drinking either."

"Well, I'm driving, so best not to."

"Toby, what would you like?"

Toby stands facing away from us.

"That man over there. Damn, he's fine!" Toby replies, and I laugh.

Toby is all talk; he never follows through. I look away as the man in his sight approaches; a tall young man, very muscular and quite good-looking. He comes to the bar but doesn't order a drink.

"Hi there, I'm Damien."

Damien is looking at me.

"Sorry, I'm here with my date,"

I reach for Toby's hand, and he takes it grudgingly.

"No worries, sorry mate," Damien nods to Toby before he moves on, and I release Toby's hand.

"Are you sure this is really a gay club? I mean, that's like the second guy who's hit on me tonight."

"Tell me about it. They're just letting everyone in," says Toby.

Choosing Me

"Who was the first?" Markus asks.

He is once again giving me his look. He sits on the stool next to me, and I spin around slowly to face him.

"The first what?" I ask.

"You said he was the second guy to hit on you. I just wondered, who was the first?" He sips his cocktail, and I notice his hand as he lifts the glass.

"The bouncer at the door asked for her number," Toby replies.

"In fact, I think that's how we managed to walk straight in without queuing, so I can't be too resentful. But seriously, what does a guy have to do to pull in a gay bar?"

Toby huffs and walks away. I jump off the stool and grab his arm.

"Where are you going?"

"Just popping to the loo, D!"

"I'm coming with you."

"To the little boy's room?"

"I can wait outside,"

I loop my arm through his.

"How about you wait right here?"

"You promised not to leave me by myself!"

"You're not by yourself; you're with Markus! Trust me, you're safe."

He removes my arm and stalks away.

"Toby!"

He can be so annoying sometimes.

I return to the bar.

"Would you like another water with lemon?"

I am a little unnerved being left alone with him, but I don't know why.

"Yes, please."

He orders my drink and gestures for me to sit on the stool next to him. Another guy approaches and starts chatting with me, but I tell him I'm on a date, and he skulks back to his corner.

"This is ridiculous!"

Choosing Me

"What is?"

"Is anyone in this club *actually* gay?"

"Toby."

"What did I do?" Toby asks.

Markus and I are both overcome with giggles.

"Toby, I'm not coming out with you anymore because you don't keep to the agreement."

"For the hundredth time, no one is plotting your murder. Honestly, you need to stop watching those 'Murder, She Wrote' reruns. Paranoid much?" says Toby while rolling his eyes.

I sip my water, smirking.

"Do you want to eat something or go straight to the club?" he asks, sipping his cocktail.

"I'm not hungry."

I am far too excited about dancing to think of food.

Markus says the same, so we head upstairs. I'm buzzing as I love to dance, but I'm always too scared to come out by myself. British men are only reserved in the daytime. At night they turn into creatures that hunt.

The girl at the door takes my jacket. My top only covers my front, so my entire back is exposed. It's a very clever design, as the hook eye over my neck creates the support, and I've tweaked it a bit to accommodate my ample bosom.

The material creates a shimmery effect and will look fabulous under the disco lights.

I'm ready. The music travels to me like a wave. We collect our wristbands, and I'm practically running inside, down the stairs, and straight to the dance floor.

The multicoloured lights and the pumping speakers jump-start my heart, transforming me into my alter ego.

I don't know who I am tonight, but when the music hits me, I move like a woman possessed.

All my inhibitions, fears, and doubts tumble to the floor. With my eyes closed and my hips swaying to the tempo of my heart, my body surrenders to the pulsating beat. I am fierce, powerful, and beautiful.

Strong arms encircle my waist and start to move in time with me. We build a rhythm of our own. I am so intent on revelling in this delight of being free, that I don't stop moving for one second.

I sense rather than see Toby coming over, but I don't stop dancing. The DJ is playing my favourite song.

"Hey, don't touch her."

"I'm just dancing, man. Just fun, no foul play."

"D, is it okay?" Toby interrupts my flow.

I turn and scan the stranger from head to toe. He looks harmless enough. He is the same height as me, covered in tattoos and piercings, but clean and kind of cute with his spiky blue mohawk. I smile.

"I'm Aries. I'm gay. I just wanted to dance with the lady. She's bad," he says to Toby.

I put my hand on Aries' chest, winking seductively, beckoning to him with my index finger. I spin around, going back to the matter at hand, taking him with me.

The music changes, and we go up-tempo. Aries can *really* move, but he lets me take the lead. With my hand on his shoulder, I smile at him, and he rocks with me to the techno beat. I throw my head back and laugh.

My prayers have been answered; the beauty of the gay dance scene. I can dance with a man and unleash my most provocative moves, not worrying about what happens after or the dreaded arousal.

We attract attention as we own the dance floor. It's infectious, and others join us, but I dance only with him. I take a break between songs, and Toby brings me mineral water from Markus.

Dancing is thirsty work, so I'm grateful. I glance up to where Markus is sitting in the private lounge area overlooking the dance floor. I can feel his eyes burning into my exposed flesh. I finish the water.

"Thank you, Toby."

I dance to the last song by myself. A flash of green is my inspiration. I could never be brave enough to

Choosing Me

take this chance for real, so I go wild with my fantasy, safe in the knowledge that it's all in my mind.

When I gyrate my hips, I envision his eyes blazing from the heat of my pulse. His sensual hands touch my body. My imagination runs wild, and the buzz intoxicates me.

My heart takes off like a rocket, but I let it happen, and when the song is finished, I taste warm tears.

I open my eyes, and he is there on his feet, looking down at me.

Making my swift escape, I run to the ladies and close the cubicle door. It's a moment before I can bring my heartbeat back to normal and stop the flow of irrational crying. I'm not sure what that was, but I wanted it to be real.

I've never fantasised about a man that I've only just met. Sweaty and breathless, I turn my attention to freshening up. My eyes are shining, and my skin is glowing.

I head back out to tell Toby I'm bushed and ready for bed. Aries gives me a high five as I stride purposefully through the throng of dancing bodies.

As I walk up the stairs in my killer stilettos, Markus does not take his eyes off me.

"Hey Toby, my feet hurt."

I sit next to him on the cool soft leather. I rest my head on his shoulders, and he puts his arm around me.

"Had fun?"

He gives me a peck on the forehead, and I nod,

"We should probably call it a night. You're doing the 10K run tomorrow."

He stands, holding me up as I slouch, "Markus, this one needs her bed. Come on, Miss Vixen, let's find you a cab."

"It was really nice to meet you, Markus, and thank you for keeping the water coming tonight."

I give him a fleeting smile, not brave enough to meet his eyes.

"I have my car, Toby; I can give her a lift."

Choosing Me

"Oh great! It's your lucky night, miss thing. D lives in the Boondocks, Markus, so it will be a bit of a long drive for you. Hope this is okay."

"Um, Toby, I'll take a cab. Thank you for the offer, Markus, but I don't want to put you out."

"It's no trouble at all," Markus replies.

He finishes his drink and puts the glass on the counter. I notice he makes sure his napkin is under the glass. I go to retrieve my jacket, and Toby comes to help me with it.

"Toby, I'm not sure about this. I know he is your friend, but he was staring at me all night," I whisper, desperate to find any excuse not to be alone in a car with him.

"Everyone was looking at you tonight. What do you expect if you go out dressed like this, shaking your wares?" says Toby.

"This outfit was pre-approved by my fashion guru, one Tobias Smith," I reply, and he grins.

"You killed it, D," he pulls me in for a hug.

I purr; Toby gives the best hugs.

"Where did Markus go?" I ask.

"He's bringing the car round. We can meet him at the back," Toby leads the way to the club's rear.

"Seriously though, Toby, who is this guy? I mean, getting a lift home from someone I don't know..." I protest, almost pleading.

"Is the taxi driver your uncle? Just chill. Me and Markus go way back. He's cool."

Toby ends any further discussion, so I shut my mouth.

A sleek black Mercedes snakes around the corner and stops alongside the curb just infront of us. Markus emerges and opens the door for me. He smiles politely, and I manoeuvre into the car in as lady-like a fashion as I can muster.

The leather seats are soft and comfortable, and the car smells of warm apples. It's very pleasant, and I immediately relax.

"Thanks again for this, Markus. Catch up with you

both tomorrow!" Toby waves, and I watch him walk away. I'm nervous again with him gone.

The car is full of gadgets and gizmos. I've no idea what any of them do, but I appreciate this is a luxury car.

"Nice car," my voice sounds a bit strange to my ears.

"Yes," he replies, "This is my favourite."

He looks over at me, the light from the dash throwing shadows on his face. The effect is beautiful, and I forget to breathe. I stare at him as if in a trance.

"Can you, uh, buckle up?" his lips move, but I don't hear him.

"What?" I reply.

"Seat belt," he gestures with his hand.

"Oh yes, of course," I recover quickly and try to put the belt around me, but I fumble with the buckle.

He reaches over to help, and as our hands touch, an electric current flows through me, and I pull my hand away. I exhale in frustration, wondering why I am a bag of nerves. Markus is occupied with his gadgets.

"What's your postcode?" his voice is composed.

I tell him and sigh in an effort to calm my nerves.

At least one of us is acting like a human.

I briefly wonder if my annoyance stems from the fact that while he is having a profound effect on me, I seem to not be affecting him much. He starts the engine.

"How long to my place?"

"We should be there in forty minutes, according to my map. Quicker if traffic is good," he winks at me.

It breaks the ice, and I laugh.

"Just don't drive like a maniac. You promised to get me home in one piece."

"You're not the adventurous type?"

"I've no issues with adventure, just as long as I make it back alive."

He laughs.

Choosing Me

"How old are you? If you don't mind my asking."

I hesitate for a moment before answering,

"I turned twenty-three last month. Why do you ask?"

"You look quite young, so I'm just checking!"

"How old do I look?" I'm not sure I want him to answer.

"It's hard to guess, but I thought you were maybe eighteen."

"Oh gosh, I really need to start acting my age."

"Your face looks really young."

"And you. How old are you?"

"Twenty-six. My next birthday is in May."

"I would've guessed older!" I glance over at him, and he is focused on the road ahead.

"Why is that, then?" he chuckles softly.

"You just seem more serious and grown up. I mean, look at this car."

It's a beautiful car, but I imagine it would suit

someone older.

"My grandpa used to drive a Mercedes," his voice is soft, so I almost don't hear him.

"So, this is your grandad's choice. What car do you like?"

I can guess he might like something elegant and sporty based on his looks.

"Fiat Coupe, fire engine red," he laughs aloud, and it sounds so good.

I laugh along with him.

"So, why do you drive this car and not a Fiat?"

"Sentimental reasons I guess, and the fact that it is a great car," his voice is tinged with sadness.

I wonder what causes those lovely green eyes to turn blue.

"Are you the sentimental type?" I ask.

"Not in every way. I tend to always throw some logic into the mix."

"I'd say that is the backbone of sound decision-making. Can I be you when I grow up?"

"What about you?" he asks.

"What about me?"

"Do you always make your own choices?"

"Absolutely. I was taught that once you're an adult, you should take control of your own life. I choose for me, always."

We both fall silent. I look at his dash. We've been driving for twenty minutes; It's past eleven. I groan as I'll have to be up in a few hours to do my charity run. I look out of the window as the city lights fly by.

His voice breaks my silent musings, "Do you work in finance with Toby?"

"Toby is more senior; he works in corporate finance. I have a junior role in the firm. I only qualified last year, but hopefully, I'll get a promotion soon."

"Do you like it?"

"You mean, did I choose to be an accountant?" I reply with a big sigh. "Well, honestly, it's plan C, but I like it well enough."

"Plan C? How is that possible? What happened to Plans A and B?"

"Hey, at least I had a plan."

"Several, by the sound of things," he says, smiling again.

"Things didn't go the way I'd hoped," I say.

"So, sometimes our choices don't quite work out," says Markus quietly.

"I guess so, but having your own free will to choose is liberating," I reply.

"I guess so," he says, but I suspect he does not agree.

"I suppose you have your whole life mapped out for you. What's the end game? Prime Minister by the tender age of thirty?"

"Not quite."

He glances at me briefly, and his face splits into a huge smile, and I notice how beautiful his teeth are. I smile back at him.

Choosing Me

"You have the most beautiful smile," he says.

"Thank you."

It's my favourite compliment.

"Seriously though, what do you do? I mean, everyone I know under the age of thirty takes the tube. They don't drive massive geriatric cars in the city."

He laughs, and I join in.

"I'm a lawyer, intellectual property specialist."

His accent is lovely.

"Fancy! But still, you would have to be a trainee or a junior. Oh, unless, of course, you're a trust fund baby?"

"I was fast-tracked as a youngster," he admits, laughing.

"Oh, not another child prodigy. I already contend with Toby. I suppose I should've known if you two were friends at school. You were probably the super brainiacs."

"Toby is the true master. He was always top of the

class. I just got lucky."

"Well, don't sell yourself short. If you're a genius, be proud of it."

"I'm not a genius. I just happen to be able to recall information without having to put in too much effort. I suppose like a photographic memory," he replies.

"I didn't think that was a real thing," I admit.

"Yes, it's real, and it can be quite annoying. Especially when you would prefer to forget."

"Oh wow, Markus, that's awesome. I guess that's why you chose to be a lawyer - lots of reading, perfect occupation."

"I wanted to be an athlete. Track and field."

"What?"

"Toby was top of the class and would annihilate me in the swimming pool, but he couldn't touch me on the track. No one could; I was fast."

"That's really cool," I say.

Toby's right. Markus is cool.

Choosing Me

I want to ask him what made him give up on his plan A but decide to keep the conversation light. I know all too well about the bitter sting of giving up on your dreams.

"And you are super lean, so I assume you still run."

"I do, mostly every day. I run in the mornings, recreationally."

"Oh, okay, stop. I'm starting to hate you. I wish I could run every day like that."

"What do you do for exercise?"

I'm tempted to say "cooking."

"I don't exercise much, even though I need to."

"How do you maintain your trim figure?"

I'm suddenly self-conscious.

"I don't. I've gained like ten pounds since I moved to London, and I'm starting to panic about it."

The confessions are flying out of my mouth. I can't seem to help myself.

"But you're running tomorrow?"

"Walking more like, but I figure I could at least lose the excess junk in my trunk," Ever the optimist, I'm hopeful.

"I blame the British winter, it's dark all day, so you hibernate and emerge seven months later as a big fat grizzly bear. In Boston, the sun shines even on very cold days."

I hear him chuckle.

"You look great, and of course, the dancing must help," he keeps his eyes on the road as we approach the junction to leave the motorway.

"Obviously, you're very attractive. You certainly attract a fair bit of attention," he adds.

I hear this often, but coming from him, it has an impact, and I am flattered that he finds me attractive, but I don't want him to know, so I roll my eyes on impulse.

"Please, from what I've seen so far, you barely need a pulse, and guys will make a move. I don't equate that to looking good. Just being human and breathing."

"Interesting theory," he says slowly.

I study his profile. He is quite handsome, but not in an obvious sort of way. I probably wouldn't have noticed him if he were not staring at me when I entered the club. He exudes an unassuming quality as if he does not wish to draw attention to himself.

My eyes travel down his torso; *his tummy is flat.*

I quickly put my hand over mine, and I sigh. No one ever notices my tummy, but it does poke out a little. I know how to hide it.

His hands barely move on the steering wheel, and my mind flashes back to my last dance tonight, fantasising about those hands on my body. He seems so capable and confident; *I like it.* Despite all the staring tonight, he hasn't actually hit on me, and I now start wondering why.

We approach a stop light, and I decide to find out what's behind those piercing stares. I smile in what I imagine is a seductive way, but I'm not sure if it works.

"Are you planning on coming down to the park tomorrow?"

He must have noticed the change. I cross my legs, and his gorgeous eyes trail up my body. I remember my tummy and start to regret this.

"Lights are green," my voice breaks his trance.

He averts his eyes and carries on driving. We are off the motorway now, so we should be at my place soon.

I wonder if he will ask for my number.

We pull up outside my apartment building, and I remove my belt and turn to him.

"Thanks so much for the lift, Markus. It was great to meet you."

"It was my pleasure."

I open my door, and he opens his door as well. This makes me stop, and I wonder what he is up to. He comes around to hold the door for me.

I thank him and attempt to step out of the car gracefully.

Choosing Me

"Perfect gentleman."

"See you tomorrow," he says softly.

I walk towards my building door and activate the key fob. His eyes follow me as I climb up the short flight of stairs. I turn, wave out the window, open my door and enter my apartment.

My heart pounds heavily in my ears, so I wait a moment to bring it back to normal. Then, I undress and head into the shower, trying not to think of my night as I wash. I send Toby a quick message and switch off my phone.

I go through my nightly ritual to prepare for bed. Fifteen minutes later, my head hits the pillow, but I can't sleep.

My mind drifts to the eyes with a lovely shade of green.

D S Johnson - Mills

Complication

Music pounds in my ear along with my heavy breathing, but I grit my teeth and jog along the road. I could swear I've been at this for ages, but the large clock in the square indicates only two hours have passed. I would be further along had I not stopped so often.

The clock is ticking. There are other colleagues here from work, and I won't be able to live this down if I'm last.

I have a stitch in my side, but I'm determined to

finish. I'm only doing ten kilometres today, but it feels like more.

Why did I agree to do this?

My legs are shaking so badly from the fatigue; it is embarrassing.

I should get more exercise; I'm so unfit.

I was the head cheer captain at my high school.

What happened to me?

I run past a girl from Marketing who is struggling more than I am. She looks like she might pass out any minute. I run on thinking to myself, *that is one silver lining*. I'm not the fainting type, never a damsel in distress.

I cross the finish line a little while later, promising myself I'll join a running club so I can keep this up. Even if I only do it from spring to late summer, it would still be something. I can go to the gym during the winter months.

Someone tells me my time: two hours and thirty minutes.

Shameful, but I'm proud. Not a bad effort for ten thirty in the morning but I'm shattered beyond belief.

I grab one of the bottles of water being handed out and drink thirstily. I look around for Toby. My feet ache so badly that I want to take off my sneakers and walk barefoot, but thankfully he sees me first.

"Hey D, high five, you did it," he looks genuinely pleased.

I give him a feeble high five.

"You did it in style too. You didn't win the race, but you get an A for the most stylish runner," he approves of my tiny red shorts and black sports top.

"I'll take it."

I sit on the bench behind him, but he pulls me up,

"You have to keep walking; you don't want to cramp up."

Toby is a volunteer today, helping to time the race and usher people toward the right areas.

"After ten mins or so, if you want to change, you can do it in one of those portacabins over there. They are the cleaner ones."

He passes me my bag.

I clean up the best I can, but I'll do the rest when I'm home. I change into a fresh pair of undies and tights with a yellow sleeveless top, which I now realise reveals way too much cleavage, but it's all I have. I leave the changing rooms, and I'm hoping we can leave to eat soon.

As I approach Toby, I can hear him chatting animatedly with someone. His back is towards me, and I can't see who he's speaking to, but judging by the way my heart rate increases, I know it's him. I put my sunglasses back on and walk over.

"Hey D, you all set?" Toby greets me, "Markus came to watch the race."

"Hey, Markus," I say, looking over at him.

He smiles at me, "Congratulations. You did a good job!"

"I did?"

"How do you feel?"

I hope I don't look as bad as I feel.

"Shattered. I ache in places I did not know were places. Starving as well. If I don't eat soon, Cruella will be showing up!"

I stand next to Toby, "Aren't you done yet?"

All this socialising will have to wait until I've been watered and fed.

"Oh, man. Markus, we need to feed her pronto. Cruella is a nasty piece of work," Toby starts packing up his bag.

I look over at Markus and smile sweetly, sipping my water. He smiles back. He is wearing sunglasses, so I cannot see his eyes. He is dressed casually in dark blue jeans, a white t-shirt, and white sneakers.

He looks very different in the daylight.

His hair is dark brown, he wears it very short and neat, and his skin is tanned like he spends a great deal of time outdoors. His face is smooth and clear, and he has a cute button nose, but his lips are the biggest surprise. He has full lips. Altogether, he is very attractive. I'm not sure why I was so nervous last night, but today, the reason has become clear – *this guy is hot stuff.* I remind myself that he didn't actually seem interested in me. Perhaps he was staring at me because he thought I was nuts. I decide to forget it and be friendly with him.

No more flirting.

Toby finishes packing up his gear. He comes over and puts his arm around me.

"Let's grab some breakfast. Markus has recommended a place not too far from here, and he has his car, so we don't have to walk."

During the short drive to the restaurant, I'm sure Markus is looking at me in the rear-view mirror, but he keeps his sunglasses on the whole time, so I have no proof.

Besides, he navigates the streets of London so expertly, there's no way he could not keep his eyes on the road.

We arrive at a restaurant on a quiet street. It looks like we're in Canary Wharf. Early on a Saturday morning, the streets are deserted. Markus holds the door open for me as I enter the restaurant, and I am tiny in my sneakers. He is smiling down at me as if he can read my thoughts.

He removes his sunglasses and asks the maître d' for a table for three. His accent is very British upper class in contrast to my harsher Bostonian twang. I realise he is well out of my league.

I'm starving, but my tummy is tied up in knots. The thought of sitting down to eat with him - his nearness - is quite daunting, and my nerves are back.

I excuse myself to go to the ladies. I want to fix my hair before I take off my cap. I wash my face and brush my hair, pulling it into a low bun. My eyes are tired, but my skin is glowing.

I head back out to the table, and as I approach, Markus stands and pulls out my chair. I accept his gesture with a thank you.

I'm wondering if his perfect gentleman routine is just the norm or exclusively for me.

I like to think it's the latter. Toby passes me the

menu, grinning slyly. I skim through the options and soon realise why.

"What is this place?" I ask, and Toby chuckles.

"No, I'm being serious. Scrambled tofu, grilled tomatoes... I don't want this!"

"It's vegan and gluten-free," Toby answers, giving me his wide-eye look.

I'm too hungry to even acknowledge him. I turn to Markus.

"I just ran a marathon, so I'm going to need more. Can I have some animal protein, please?"

Toby is cracking up, "Please, D, you did a ten-kilometre run and walked most of the way. That's not a marathon."

I reward him with one of my looks and almost growl.Markus is very amused, but I'm not impressed.

"What would you like?" he asks me.

"Cheeseburger, no bun, with sauteed mushrooms and, if possible, a lemon and ginger smoothie, please," I reply in my sweetest voice.

Markus signals for the waiter, and he is rewarded with a smile from me.

"Are you always vegan, or is it just today?" I'm feeling grateful.

"Not always. Since I was fourteen."

"Now, don't take this the wrong way. I say this with the utmost respect, but why?"

"How do I put this? I've always been sensitive about consuming animals."

"Wow! Is this the real reason Toby always beats you in the swimming pool? You were hungry?"

"Is that what he told you?" Markus' eyes narrow as he looks at Toby.

"No, I did not tell her that," Toby replies.

"Tobes, what did you order?"

"A grilled cheese sandwich with fries," he grins.

"I come here to eat quite often as they have a good vegan selection, but they do have a non-vegan menu."

"And you, Markus?"

Choosing Me

There is nothing appealing on the menu.

"Waffles with banana and berry mix," he replies.

"Doesn't that need milk, butter, and eggs?" I challenge.

"They use non-dairy options and definitely no eggs," he fires back.

He's obviously used to being questioned about his diet. Sheesh, how miserable to never be able to lick your plate. The waiter shows up with my smoothie, and I drink it in one go.

"Take it easy," Toby cautions me.

"Sorry, I'm thirsty, and that was *so* good. Why was it so small?" I look at Markus.

"I hope the food doesn't come in such tiny portions," I speak up just as the food arrives.

I spend the next ten minutes eating.

"Mm, so good," I say between bites.

Markus is watching me as he chews his waffles.

"She also makes sounds while eating," Toby tells

him, giving me his 'I can't take you anywhere' look.

"Oh, come on, Toby."

"Yes, I know. You ran a marathon today!" he rolls his eyes, and we all start to laugh.

"Are you two like this at work?" Markus asks, shaking his head.

I watch in fascination as he chews his food. His moves are mechanical, his waffles are stacked neatly on his plate, and he slices a bite-size amount, puts it in his mouth, and chews slowly. I have no clue if he is enjoying his food.

On the other hand, I have already finished my meat and mushrooms and I'm eyeing up Toby's grilled cheese sandwich. He breaks a piece and puts it on my plate.

"Thank you!" I pop it into my mouth and chew slowly, washing it down with the rest of my smoothie.

"No," I say, answering Markus's question,

"Toby works in the posh offices upstairs, and I'm not allowed to visit unless invited. He even has an office with his name on the door; 'Tobias Smith, Head of Corporate Finance, Northern Europe Division'."

Toby looks at me like I'm nuts, but he laughs.

"I do sometimes daydream about having my name on a door one day. I can see it now. 'Dylan Weekes, Head of All Things Nonsensical'."

Toby is falling off his chair, laughing, and I join in.

"Who's Dylan?" Markus asks.

Toby and I both stare at him.

"I am. I'm Dylan."

"I thought your name was Dee."

Toby has now lost all sense of reason and is cracking up.

"Behave, Toby," I say, trying to feign annoyance but failing.

"Toby introduced you as Dee last night, so I assumed... I do apologise."

I extend my hand towards him.

"Dylan Francine Weekes, pleased to make your acquaintance."

He takes my hand briefly, but butterflies flood my stomach, and I almost gasp.

Does he feel the same? His face gives nothing away.

"Toby likes to take shortcuts."

"I apologise too," Toby adds, fully recovered from his laughing spell, "I do sometimes forget myself. I call her D, but it is short for Dylan."

The waiter appears and asks if all is okay. He probably heard our cackling. We've finished eating, so Markus asks for the bill. He refuses to let us contribute, so we end up leaving the waiter a huge tip.

Standing up to leave, my right calf muscle spasms, and I fall back in my chair.

I grab Toby's arm, "Toby, my legs are burning!"

"Lactic acid. You need to start moving. You've been sitting too long."

He holds on to me and helps me up. Markus

helps with my bag, and we head out into the sunshine.

"I guess I should've trained, huh?"

"You think?" Toby replies.

My legs are like concrete blocks, stiff and unyielding; I can barely move them. The car is not far away, but each step is excruciating.

"Can you climb on my back? I'll help you to the car," Toby offers.

"I could try, but, Tobes, I weigh a ton!"

"Come on, woman, just do it!"

He bends over, and I hop on and laugh as he grabs me and swears, "A ton? An elephant is lighter than you, my God!"

I look over at Markus, and he is laughing at us. I am a bit self-conscious as my top has lifted, and too much of me is exposed. I hold on for dear life.

I try to adjust my top, but Markus pulls it down for me. The moment feels very intimate as his fingers graze the soft skin on my stomach.

"Thank you."

"You're welcome," he replies.

We make it to the car in one piece. The sweet smell of apples invades my senses.

"Where can you drop us, Markus? I can go to the station, then make my way home," I say as he holds the door open for me.

I climb into the front while Toby is in the back seat, complaining that I have damaged his back. Markus closes the door and goes round to the driver's side.

"I don't mind. I can drop you home," he offers.

He turns to look at Toby, who is busy texting on his Blackberry.

"Where're you heading, Toby?" Markus asks.

"I'm okay to be dropped at the station. I'm making a detour."

Markus starts the engine, and I'm so grateful for the lift. I'm exhausted. We drop Toby off at Canning Town station.

"Thanks, mate," says Toby, stepping out of the

car.

"D, I'll call you later. Take care of my girl Markus!"

Toby waves and disappears into the Saturday crowd, and I briefly wonder where he is off to.

With Toby gone from the car, the air becomes electric. I'm aware of every move Markus makes. He is quiet as he drives. The traffic is quite heavy, not like last night, and I think he will soon become frustrated, but he remains calm.

"I think traffic is going to be bad at this time on a Saturday. Honestly, I can just take the train home," I say half-heartedly.

"It's heavy but not too bad. You'll be home quicker this way."

I lean back in the seat.

"I don't want to take up so much of your time. In case you had plans."

He glances over at me and smiles.

"No plans," he says, "An ice bath will help with the pain," he adds.

"For me, those two words shouldn't even be said together," I shudder at the thought.

"I suppose not," he chuckles.

He's right. The traffic is heavy, but it is moving, and before long, we're on the motorway.

I must have drifted off as the next moment, the car stops.

"You're home," Markus' voice wakes me from my slumber.

The car is in the same bay as last night.

"Is it okay to park here?" he asks.

"Yes, this is my spot. I'm number twenty-seven," I reply.

He comes round to open my door and helps with my bag. I move to step out of the car, but my legs have decided not to work. I'm seized by panic, worried that he will have to carry me up the stairs.

I hold on to the car door and move my legs, willing them to take me inside my apartment. I grit my teeth, forcing my legs to cooperate. The pain is intense, but

Choosing Me

I ignore it.

"My keys are in the bag," I say, and he passes me my bag.

I retrieve the keys and open the door to my building.

Twelve steps will take me to my apartment, my heart sinks.

I glance over my shoulder at Markus, and he is watching me.

"Is it okay if I help you?" he offers.

I groan as I'm mortified.

"If you keep moving, it'll be easier. Once you stop, your muscles freeze up."

I take his advice. I start to move on the spot, and after a minute or so, I take the stairs two at a time. It does work. I enter my apartment, and Markus stands at the door. I wait for him to tell me that he is leaving, but his eyes meet mine, and I realise I don't want him to go.

"You can come in."

He enters my apartment.

I remove my sneakers and place them on the small shoe rack by my door. He does the same. I smile, relieved. My home is a shoe-free zone.

"Your apartment is quite nice."

"I'm going to shower and change. Make yourself comfortable. Kitchen and lounge are that way," I gesture to the right, as my bedroom is on the left.

There's another bedroom at the end of the hallway. This place is my castle. I hear him filling up the kettle.

After a hot shower, my body hums with relief. I think the nap in the car helped. My muscles are achy, but I'm freshly washed and home. I dress in blue cotton shorts and a white halter neck top. When I join him in the lounge, he is looking at my photographs. He holds a framed photo of me and my sister, taken a few months ago.

"Hey."

"I hope you don't mind," he says, holding up the

picture.

"Your sister?"

"Yes, New Year's Eve party back home. It was so much fun. We thought it was our last night before the millennium, so we decided to dress up to the max and go out with a bang," I laugh, remembering.

"You look alike," he says.

"Really? Most people say she is like my dad."

In the photograph, we do have identical smiles. I never noticed it before.

"She's quite pretty," he says softly, "You both look so young. Is she back in Boston?"

He stands close, and suddenly, breathing becomes a chore, so I move away. My heart is racing. I open my windows to let some air in. I turn back to face him, and his eyes meet mine.

"Yes," I say to answer his question.

"You must miss your family."

"I do, but I visit them often, so it's not so bad," I shrug.

He replaces the frame and looks at another picture of me with my dad.

"What about your mother?"

"She lives in New York," I mumble.

"Did you boil the kettle?" I quickly change the subject, not wanting to talk about my mother.

"Yes, I made peppermint tea. Would you like one?"

"No thanks."

I move over to sit on the couch, but it takes me a while as my legs resist. Moving cautiously before giving up, I gasp as my thigh muscles go into another spasm.

"Crap!" I say too loudly, "I think something is torn."

Markus is suddenly near me, with heat radiating from his body.

"You, alright?"

His voice is close to my ear, and his hand is on my shoulder. Blood is pulsing where his hand rests lightly, and I wonder, *if he touched my thighs, would it help to alleviate the pain?*

I glance at his hand, and he removes it. He helps me on to the couch and then sits next to me.

"I'm good. No pain, no gain!"

The pulse in my neck throbs painfully. I'm conscious he might notice, so I reach out to grab my phone, fidgeting with the buttons nervously.

"I'd forgotten to text Toby that I was home. I'll just do it now."

I fire off the message, and am about to put my phone away, when I turn to him.

"Hey Markus, can I have your number?" I raise one eyebrow, "I can dial a ride in case I'm ever stranded in the city," I laugh, giving him my best smile.

"May I?" he asks.

He reaches out to take my phone. I notice his hands. His fingers are long and slender, his nails short and clean.

They're beautiful.

I realise that I may be into hands. Toby has nice ones too.

He dials a number from my phone, and his Blackberry starts to buzz. He ends the call, dials the number back, and his number flashes on my screen. He saves it to my contacts.

"Should I save your number as D or Dylan?" he asks, smiling at me.

"Up to you. I answer to both names these days."

"How're your legs feeling?"

I wonder if he likes my legs. I know they're pretty good; I receive compliments all the time.

He looks at me, and I've no clue what he's thinking.

His face gives nothing away.

"A bit better."

"They'll hurt tomorrow. Try not to sit for long periods of time. Maybe go out for a walk."

I could listen to his voice all day.

Suddenly, I'm consumed by the urge to kiss him.

Would he like that or be repulsed by it? How much time should you wait to kiss someone you barely know?

I've no clue what the rules of dating are. I've not been kissed in a while. The last time was not that great, either.

"Would you like more tea?" I ask.

"Yes, please."

Taking his advice to move more, I stand slowly, groaning as my legs protest, shuffling to the kitchen. My muscles do feel less achy once I am up. I make two cups of tea. The aroma from the peppermint invades my senses as I place a coaster neatly under the cups on the coffee table.

"Thank you, Dylan."

I sit on the arm of the couch, as it is much easier than trying to sink back onto the cushioned seat. I remove my flip-flops, turn my legs around to face him, and rest my bare feet on the sofa.

"You're welcome, Markus."

My name sounds good on his lips.

We both lock eyes for a moment, and I am sure he is attracted to me.

My phone rings, and it breaks the spell. It's Toby. Surprisingly, I'm annoyed that he's calling me now. This is a first. I'm always happy to hear from him.

"Hey, Toblerone," I answer on the second ring, "What do you want?" My eyes are still locked on Markus.

I should ask Toby what to do.

"Just checking on you," he replies.

"My legs ache, but I'm coping."

"They'll hurt more tomorrow," he says.

"Don't worry about me. I'll survive, but I'm not sure if I can come to the market with you tomorrow."

"Alright, D, no worries. I'll catch up with you on Monday for lunch. Take care of yourself," he rings off.

Choosing Me

I hang up and throw the phone onto a nearby chair.

I turn to Markus, "Did Toby date any guys when you were at school together?"

"I don't know," he replies, and I'm a bit disappointed.

They've known each other for so long, and I thought he would know for sure.

He doesn't look at me when he replies. It's a bit weird.

I try a different question, "Did you always know he was gay?"

"No, but sexual preferences can develop later," he speaks slowly and carefully.

"He seems to like you a lot," he adds.

"I love him to bits, which is unusual for me as there are not a lot of people I can be myself with. But it's so easy with Tobes; I don't even think about it,"

I smile, thinking about my good friend.

"I never see him with anyone, and it just makes

me wonder why."

"Ask him. I'm sure he'll tell you," Markus replies.

"I know. I think I'm afraid of what he'll say," I admit.

"Why?"

"Toby and I, we have an unspoken rule. We don't talk about each other's sex life, but I worry that one day he'll meet someone, and then things will be different."

"You might meet someone as well," he says softly.

The light shines into the window turning his eyes a light shade of green, and they pierce through me. I look away, focusing on the untouched cups on my coffee table.

"My tea!"

He moves to bring it to me, still gazing at me in his way.

I sip, and it's still warm. I gobble it down in one go and give him back the cup as he is waiting for it. I thank him in a chirpy voice.

Choosing Me

He smiles and goes to put the cup away. He sips his tea slowly, and I laugh.

Markus excuses himself to use my loo. I think about him while he is gone. I have a large mirror on my wall adjacent to the dining table, and I look over at myself. My top reveals my cleavage, and I wonder if he notices.

Maybe he has a girlfriend. That would make sense.

When he returns, I think he is going to tell me that he is leaving, but he takes his seat on the couch and smiles at me, so I make my move.

"What about you?" I ask, feeling brave.

"What about me?" he returns my smile.

He does that a lot.

"Did you date any guys at school?" I ask, smiling coyly at him.

"No, I didn't," he answers, laughing, showing off his beautiful teeth, "I'm not gay," his eyes flicker to my cleavage, and he glances away just as quickly.

"Well, I don't know. I met you in a gay club, and you haven't tried anything with me."

"Maybe I'm just being the perfect gentleman."

"Markus, do you have a girlfriend?"

"It's complicated."

Choosing Me

Impulsive

My eyes fall to his lips, full and enticing. His eyes meet mine, and in that moment, I decide to kiss him. If only to feel his lips against mine, just once.

"Is there any way to uncomplicate the situation?"

"I can only see the situation becoming more complicated."

"I don't know why people complicate things. If anything in my life makes me feel that way, I just cut it loose."

"Choices, right?" His voice is soft, and I nod in agreement.

"Absolutely! I want to always be free to go after whatever I want."

"What if the thing you want is unattainable?" he whispers, his eyes boring into mine.

"At least I would have tried."

I'm not sure if I sound brave or foolish.

I decide to put my money where my mouth is. I slowly inch off the arm of the couch and move over to where he's sitting. My heart is racing, and I'm terrified. He watches as I move closer, but he doesn't move an inch. I sit back on my legs, no longer caring about the pain, and I take his right hand in mine. His hands are soft.

My fingertips graze his palm slowly, and I entwine my fingers with his. He closes his eyes and exhales. Encouraged by this tiniest of reactions, I lean forward and softly touch my lips to his, pressing firmer.

His left hand moves up the side of my arm to

caress my neck. His featherlight touch is like silk against my smooth skin. I moan softly, and open to taste more. He kisses me back.

I expect a first kiss to be slow, but this kiss is quite ferocious. His mouth is warm, sweet from the mint tea, and our breath mingles. He takes control of the kiss. His hand goes to the back of my head, and he pulls me closer.

Our tongues touch, and I lose my composure.

I've never been kissed in this way. I surprise myself by letting go and falling into the sensations, new and thrilling, throwing my arms around his neck and moulding my chest to his.

His hand moves slowly up my back, caressing my skin expertly. I'm aroused and panting, breathing heavily. It's embarrassing as he makes no sound.

With trembling fingers, I unbutton the top of my halter neck. He groans and deepens the kiss, drinking me in.

His reaction spurs me on. I break the kiss, remove my top impulsively and throw it on the floor. I'm not wearing a bra. He freezes, but I'm in too deep now. I take his hand and put it over my swollen breast. My nipples are like hard pebbles. I close my eyes and moan from the sensations running through my body.

"Kiss me," I whisper.

His warm mouth on my pulsating nipples leaves me breathless. This is erotic. I don't want him to stop, but to my everlasting embarrassment, I climax. My leg muscles scream from pain, and my breasts are sensitive from his kisses and caresses. He's not being very gentle.

I cry out, and he stops. He breathes heavily, and it's a while before he breathes normally again. I cover my breasts with my arms.

"Sorry," I whisper, mortified at my actions.

He retrieves my top from the floor, and I quickly try to put it over my head. He reaches out to help me. I'm so ashamed; I want to cry.

I move to the furthest corner of the sofa and don't look him in the eye. He must be thinking I'm easy.

Choosing Me

I want to die.

"Dylan?" he says my name and softly touches my leg.

I fight the urge to push his hand away.

"You, okay?" he asks.

"Yes. I'm sorry. I'm not sure why I did that," tears sting my eyes.

My hair has come loose from its bun and is a bit messy, so I try to tame it. Markus helps me. He locates my hair slide and pulls my hair back into the bun. I smile to thank him.

"Don't be sorry," he whispers, smoothing my hair.

I finally look at him, "Markus, are you attracted to me?"

His eyes narrow for a split second; I think my question has confused him.

"Yes, I am. Very much so," he runs his hand down my arm, "Isn't it obvious?"

He takes my hand.

"No," I pull my hand away, "It's not obvious to me."

"Dylan, what's wrong?"

"I don't like to play my hand first," I pout.

He smiles, leans over, and kisses me on the mouth. I don't resist, and I let him touch me. The kiss deepens, and he groans. He pulls away and kisses me softly on my swollen lips.

"You should do it more often; it's very sexy. Besides, I wanted to give you a choice. I know how important that is to you."

"Where'd you learn to kiss like that?" I ask softly.

"When I was fifteen, I had my first kiss. I stuck my tongue in her mouth. She told me that it wasn't nice and showed me how she wanted to be kissed instead," he says, laughing.

"Sounds like a bad-ass fifteen-year-old girl."

"Sixteen, actually. She was older."

"Seduced by an older woman? I'm both shocked and impressed."

Choosing Me

"She's the complication."

"Why?" I whisper, running my fingers up and down his palm.

"You want to know why I didn't ask you out before? She's why."

"So, you do have a girlfriend?"

"We're separated," he whispers.

"What's so complicated about that?"

"I've known her for twelve years."

"Twelve years. You've been in a relationship for that long?"

I may be in over my head here. My first and only relationship lasted less than a year.

"Yes, on and off," he admits, closing his eyes.

"Wow, why did you break up?"

"We both want different things," he admits.

"Do you love her?"

"Yes," he whispers, and I understand that I've now swanned in with my perky boobs to complicate things even more.

"Sorry," I whisper, "I'll make it my mission from now on to ensure that there will be no further kissing, inappropriate touching, wardrobe malfunctions, or displaying of boobs."

I put his beautiful hand back in his lap and move back to the arm of the couch. This move exposes my legs, and I try to adjust myself.

"You have the most beautiful legs," he says, "In fact, there's not much about you that I don't find sexy."

It's so ironic how I wanted him when he wasn't hitting on me, and now that he is, I want him to stop. He's in love with another woman, and I don't want to come in between that.

"Markus, let's just be friends, okay? I don't want to make things more complicated for you."

I'm being quite genuine. I don't like to be the cause of anyone being unhappy. It's one of my most redeeming qualities. He stares at me for a long time and exhales.

Choosing Me

My stomach growls.

"I'm hungry," my insides feel hollow.

"Me too," he responds, "Do you want to grab some food?"

This sounds like a "friendly" thing to do.

"Sure, I'll change my clothes," I move slowly off the arm of the couch.

He helps me, and I smile as a thanks.

I dress in a grey cotton fitted top, ensuring to wear my bra and tight blue jeans. I braid my hair to make it look tidy, apply mascara and lip gloss, and grab my purse and leather jacket. My wedged heel boots give me extra height.

"Ready," I call him from my hallway.

Markus appears and appraises me. That fiery burn is back in his eyes, and I have a pang of guilt for lighting it in the first place.

"Where are we going to eat?"

"I know somewhere."

He helps me into my jacket.

"You look very sexy," he whispers, kissing my neck.

I guess I brought this on myself, so I let him do it, but when he releases me, I turn to him.

"Markus, we're going to be friends now, so that's not so appropriate anymore," I admonish as if he's a small child.

He smiles and kisses me on the mouth, and I exhale as he puts on his sneakers.

He takes me to an Indian restaurant somewhere in Shoreditch. I'd never come to this part of London knowingly as it looks quite dangerous. As he parks the car, a heady mix of graffiti, litter, and grungy old buildings loom ominously.

It gives me the creeps.

He opens my car door, and we walk hand in hand to the restaurant. I allow him to hold my hand as I'm a bit worried that we might be mugged. We join a long queue, but he tells me the food is worth the wait. His eyes blaze as he says this, and it makes me laugh.

"Are you sure the car's okay?" I ask once we are seated in the restaurant.

"We'll soon find out," he's amused at my cowardice.

"What would you like to eat? They have a good selection here, and the food is the best."

He seems different, changed somehow. Happy and relaxed.

It's infectious, and soon I'm chatting and eating the most delicious food.

Did we only just meet yesterday? It seems like I have known Markus for ages.

He doesn't mention his complication anymore, and I don't pry. He asks me about my life in London and how long I've known Toby. He tells me about his Grandpa Joe and all the times they went hiking in Scotland and Switzerland, and about his time working in Spain, for his law firm, which he enjoyed.

"There's a chance I might go back as they still

haven't found anyone to run things there. The Spanish employees want to work in London," he says.

"When?"

I swallow a pang of disappointment and caution myself not to become attached.

"I'm not sure; we're currently recruiting, so if that goes well, I won't be needed," he replies.

"I guess your Spanish has to be impeccable!" I smile.

"Si, mi Española es suficientemente bueno."

I stare at his mouth as he speaks Spanish with a British accent. I suddenly feel nugatory. I wondered if he was out of my league earlier today, and now, I truly believe this to be the case. An old ache flares deep in the pit of my stomach, but I stifle it down.

"Hey, can I pay for dinner since you paid for breakfast?"

"Sure, but who is going to pay for the cab fare home if the car is no longer there?"

"I will. You've been chauffeuring me around for

two days now. I think I owe you."

"Dylan, you don't owe me anything. It was my pleasure," he whispers the last part, and I try not to meet his eyes but fail.

We stare at each other. Our waitress comes to check on us, and the moment is broken. When she brings us the bill, my eyes go wide.

"You're just eating plants. How can it be so expensive?" I say, feigning mock horror, so he laughs.

I freshen up in the ladies' room before we leave and check if I look okay.

"He's not available," I say to myself in the mirror.

The irony is not lost on me. I finally meet a guy who ticks all the boxes but one, the most important one. I touch my lips, remembering the sweetness of his on mine, and apply more lip-gloss.

Markus waits patiently. His eyes travel up my body as I approach. He smiles, reaching to take my hand, and I don't pull away. We leave to go back out into zombie land, and I want to hurry to the car.

"Do you want to wait at the restaurant? I can bring the car around."

"No way. Who's going to watch your back?" I ask, and he laughs aloud, "Hush, don't lead them right to us," I whisper.

I walk faster despite my achy muscles.

"I was hoping to give you a piggyback ride to the car, but you seem to be coping well," he grins.

"It's pure adrenaline that's keeping me going. I'll feel it later, but that's okay with me."

I break into a run. He holds the door open, and I climb inside as quickly as I can. It's dark and cold outside.

Markus starts the car and puts on the heaters.

"Are you warm enough?" he reaches over to touch my hands.

"I'm warm. Let's get the hell out of here."

He chuckles and drives out of the parking lot. His clock displays eleven-thirty; I can't believe how quickly the day has gone. It's been so eventful, but I'm

Choosing Me

starting to become quite apprehensive that it'll be over soon.

He pulls into my parking bay, turns off the ignition, and comes around to help me out.

I fumble for my keys in my bag. He takes them from my trembling fingers and opens the door activating the fob. He helps me up the stairs one step at a time, unlocking my apartment door, and we go in.

I'm so nervous I don't look at him. Waiting with bated breath for the moment when he will tell me he is leaving. My reaction surprises me, but I tell myself it's probably because I know that nothing can happen between us.

"I'm going to go home now. Will you be alright?"

I don't respond but look up, staring at his mouth.

"I can help you to bed if you want," he offers.

"I can manage," I smile, "I had a really nice day."

We don't speak for a while.

"Can I see you tomorrow?" he asks softly.

"I don't think that's a good idea."

"Not even as friends?"

"I usually go to the Sunday Market with Toby, but I already cancelled that. If he finds out I went out with you, he might be a bit put out." I laugh, but he just looks at me, so I sigh.

"What were you thinking we could do?" I ask, giving in.

I look down at my hands as I speak. I look up when he does not respond, and our eyes lock.

"How about I pick you up and see where the day takes us?" he whispers, and I nod.

His emerald eyes light up when he smiles, and I smile back at him. He bends down and plants a chaste kiss on my lips.

"Goodnight, Dylan. Sleep well."

He opens my door and closes it behind him, and I exhale.

"Dylan, what have you done?"

Choosing Me

Proposition

The next morning shines bright and sunny. I'm up early in anticipation of the day ahead. I wash my hair and dry it, but it goes frizzy. I call the local hairdressers to see if they can flat iron it for me. I have work tomorrow, so I'd like it to look sleek. They squeeze me in, so I jump in a cab and head out to resolve the issue that is my hair.

When I resemble a human again, I take another cab to the supermarket to stock up on non-dairy milk. The choices are endless. I pick one brand and hope for the best.

Markus texted me last night and said I should let him know when I was ready, no doubt thinking I wanted to sleep in. While I'm queuing to pay, I message him to pick me up in an hour.

I take the short walk home. My legs are still sore from yesterday's excursion, but not unbearably so. Markus was right. The more I move, the better they feel. I have no clue how to dress as I've no idea where we are going.

I'm excited but also want to be good, so I dress as if I'm going out with Toby, in fitted blue jeans and a yellow striped sweater. I'll decide on the shoes based on what he's wearing. I've never mastered the art of applying foundation, so I usually go without it, but I'm wondering now if my café au lait complexion is too pale.

I go outside to put the rubbish out, and he pulls up. He is wearing jeans, a light green sweater over a white t-shirt, and black sneakers.

"Hello," he says, smiling, "How are you?"

Choosing Me

He walks towards me and kisses my lips. I don't address the kiss because it's quite nice. He reaches out to touch my hair.

"Hello yourself, I'm good."

"You look gorgeous. Did you change your hair?"

"I had to wash it."

"It looks great."

I think I must have "the talk" with him again; our boundaries are becoming blurry.

"Where are we off to today?" I ask over my shoulder as I slowly walk up the stairs.

He follows behind me.

"Cambridge," he says, and I stop at the top of the stairs.

We collide, and he grabs me around my waist to steady us. I gasp from the unexpected heat radiating between our bodies.

"Cambridge?" I ask breathlessly, moving quickly away from those hands to open the door.

"Yes, so wear comfy shoes, lots of walking today."

"I did lots of walking yesterday."

He laughs boyishly. He's in such happy spirits.

The roads are empty, and we arrive in record time. Markus parks in the city centre; it's a stark contrast to the car park last night.

The colleges are seeping with history, and we walk through their grounds, holding hands. The sky is a cloudless, deep blue shade, providing a postcard backdrop against the magnificent buildings.

"Would you like to visit the chapel? It's just up ahead."

"Do you come here often?"

"No, I haven't been here since my Uni days."

"You studied at Cambridge University?"

"Yes," he replies.

"I'm a Yale alumna," I say, "Well, let me retract that. I only did the first year in Connecticut, and then I dropped out."

Choosing Me

"Why?"

"Long story. I majored in psychology, and let's just say it was messing with my head. I came to London on holiday, fell in love, and decided to stay for a bit. I enrolled at City."

We arrive at the small chapel facing the river. He smiles at me as I babble, so I stop talking.

"Would you like to go in?" he asks, and I nod.

The Chapel doorway is very low, and he bends his head. It's eerily quiet and peaceful inside. We sit at an empty pew.

I think the service must have just ended.

The air is electric, but I know it's because he is close to me.

I fight the urge to reach out and touch him; I cross my legs, wedging my hands between my thighs. He runs his hands down my hair, and I exhale, closing my eyes.

His touch is exquisite.

We gaze into each other's eyes, then he bends his

head, and his lips touch mine.

What happened yesterday was not my imagination; the sensation of his full lips against mine is pure pleasure. Sitting inside a holy chapel, kissing a man who may or may not belong to someone else does not bring on the sinful condemnation one would expect. Nevertheless, I break away.

"Let's go," he whispers.

We eat lunch at a quaint restaurant overlooking the canal.

"Would you like to go out on the river?" he asks.

"I'd love to."

"I once went punting with Toby in Oxford, but he was slightly tipsy. He couldn't steer the boat, so I ended up doing it."

"Why don't you drink alcohol?"

"I don't like the idea of being intoxicated. I saw too many drunk students in my first year of Uni, and It turned me off."

"One glass of wine won't render you drunk."

Choosing Me

"I've no idea what my limit is?"

"Would you like to find out?"

"No. I'm good, thank you."

"Are you ready?"

"Yes, sure."

The boat sways gently as the oars move in sequence through the murky waters. It's peaceful out on the river. He rows along, pointing out where he used to study and the common room.

"Did you live on campus?"

"No. I lived in the city centre. I was seventeen, so it wasn't allowed for me to live on campus the first year."

"Was it difficult for you to make friends being so much younger?"

"No. I looked older than my years. I have an old man's face. You said that to me as well."

"I didn't say that. I was referencing more to your mannerisms. You're poised and exude confidence, so it makes you seem older. You have a beautiful face."

He stares at me, and I stop laughing, concentrating on the scenery floating by, but I can feel his eyes on me. There are a few other punters on the river, and they say hello. I smile and wave politely.

"I want to show you something, Dylan."

He veers off until we come to a small jetty. He ties up the boat and jumps out. He offers me his hand, and I step out. He has a small backpack, and we go on a short hike along the river until we come to a small, picturesque garden with blooming daffodils.

"Markus, this is lovely."

He removes a blanket from his bag, spreads it down on the grass, and gestures for me to sit. I oblige. He removes his sneakers, and I do the same, enjoying the gentle breeze on my toes. The sun's rays shine through the trees. I close my eyes, sighing contentedly, holding my face and neck up to the sun. My pulse begins to race, as I can tell that he is still watching me.

"How're your legs feeling?"

Choosing Me

"They hurt, but the walking helps."

"Do you wish you had gone to the market with Toby?"

"I do miss it, but it's nice being here. I've always wanted to come."

"Can I ask you something?" he speaks softly, and I nod my head, sighing contentedly.

"How is it you don't have a boyfriend?"

I open my eyes; this is not what I was expecting him to ask.

"I don't know what I'm looking for yet. Besides, I was busy studying and settling into London life."

"So, you haven't been with anyone since moving to the UK?"

"No, I haven't."

"Is there someone back in Boston?"

I shake my head. He frowns, so I decide to tell him.

"I was engaged. We were at Yale together."

"I'm sorry, Dylan. I don't mean to pry."

"It's alright. I asked about your life, so it's only fair."

He doesn't question me about this anymore. We talk about other things, and the rest of the time goes by quickly. The clouds cover the sun, and the day turns grey and cold. He holds my hand as we walk back to the car. We talk and laugh easily on the drive back to my place. He pulls the car into my spot and helps me up the stairs. My fingers refuse to comply as I try to pry my door open.

"Is it okay if I come in?" he asks.

"Markus, I...."

"Hey, Dylan!"

I glance over my shoulder at the sound of my name and notice my next-door neighbour coming inside the communal door and joining us in the hallway. Her eyes go wide when she sees Markus.

"Hey, Cynthia."

The hallway is crowded, so I gesture for Markus

to go inside.

I make small talk before telling her I must go. She gives me two thumbs up, and I smile.

He stands just inside the door. I lose my train of thought when he looks at me with those eyes.

"I'm just going to change my clothes," I say.

He nods and goes off to the lounge.

I shower, slip on a form-fitting mini-dress with long sleeves, and brush out my hair. The warm water helps to calm my nerves. I come out of my bedroom as he leaves the bathroom.

"Would you like tea or coffee? I bought non-dairy milk."

"Sure. I'll have tea, please," he says, eyeing me up. "Nice dress."

I pretend not to hear him. I make his tea and place it next to where he sits on the couch. Leaving distance between us, I stand by the dining table across from him at the other end of the room. His eyes travel up my body, lingering on my legs.

"Why do you always shower and change when you come home?"

"What do you mean?" I know what he means, but I act coy.

"You always change your clothes as soon as you walk through the door. You did it yesterday and now today."

"No special reason."

It is way too early to share my obsession with everything clean.

"Can I see you again tomorrow?"

"I have work."

"I thought I could pick you up after, and we could do something."

I shake my head to protest, but he stands and takes my hand. He pulls me over to the couch and kisses me. I'm caught off guard and swept up in the pressure of his lips. I know I should stop this, but I don't. I press myself against him. His hand is in my hair, running down my back. His touch is like fire, and I smoulder. His hand goes under my dress and touches my bare legs.

"No," I whisper, and he stops.

It's a moment before I can speak again. I move to the arm of the chair and adjust my dress.

"I'm sorry," I say.

"Don't apologise. It's perfectly alright," he replies.

"I do want to…," I whisper softly.

He comes closer and lifts me onto his lap. He smooths my hair, and we sit like this for a while. My heart races. His arousal presses hard against my thigh, and I want to move off his lap, but I stay put.

I'm not sure how we start kissing again, but this time, I take his hand and put it under my dress. I'm past the point of control; I pant and moan, wanting more as my body ignites.

Throwing caution to the wind, I stand and remove my dress, dropping it to the floor. His pupils appear to dilate at the sight of me in my bra and panties. I resist my rational thoughts.

Moving swiftly, I sit astride him, moulding my lips to his and tasting his sweet breath.

Rubbing the softness of my thighs against his erection, I'm blinded with pleasure.

"I want you," I say breathlessly.

He kisses me deeply, and his hands go to my fleshy derriere, pulling me onto him. I gyrate my hips. His fingers slip inside the straps of my panties, and I freeze. I'm shaking so hard. The reality of what is happening finally comes home to me. I stand up and away from his lap, struggling to pull enough oxygen into my body.

"Dylan?"

"I'm fine," I choke out.

He takes my dress off the floor and walks to the kitchen, bringing me water, which I drink, even though my hands shake uncontrollably. He takes the glass back to the kitchen, helps me slip into my dress, and pulls me into his arms.

"I'm sorry. I've never gone all the way before. I

just panicked."

"What do you mean?" he takes my shaking hands in his.

My fingers are cold, and his are warm.

"I haven't..." I whisper, hiding my face in his chest.

"Are you a virgin?"

I simply nod my head, finally looking up at him. I move slowly to sit on the arm of the couch, wincing slightly as my leg muscles burn. He stands staring at me.

He comes out of his momentary trance and sits next to me.

"How is it possible that you've never had sex? What about your fiancé?"

"He never pressured me for sex. I knew he wanted to, and we did try, but...."

His eyes bore into mine, and I cannot finish. Shame consumes me, still, after all these years. I stare at the bulge in his trousers, willing it not to disappear, never wanting to relive the humiliation.

"What happened when you tried?"

"I think maybe I didn't turn him on," I whisper my words, not wanting to say them out loud.

"That's not possible."

"He would always go soft, but he said it was because I didn't really want to. I thought about it, being with him, but for whatever reason, I just... couldn't."

He pulls me onto his lap and stares into my eyes before his lips touch mine ever so lightly. I close my eyes and move in for more. He runs his hands over my hair but does not kiss me, so I open my eyes.

"I'd like my first time to be with you."

He exhales but does not respond. Undeterred, I press my lips against his. I try to copy the way he kisses me. He moans, and the sounds go through me, sending shockwaves into my body. I cling to him, wanting more.

"Are you sure?" he asks, breaking the kiss.

"Yes, but only if you want to," I whisper, going in

Choosing Me

for more.

"I want to."

"What about how you feel about your complication?"

"We have history, and I care very deeply for her; I probably always will."

I like that he is being honest with me.

"Do you think you two will reconcile? It sounds like there are still a lot of feelings between you."

"Honestly, I hope not. My only wish is for her to be happy."

We're both silent. He looks at me, and I look at him. I reach out and take his hand in mine. I want to ask him more questions about the woman he loves, but he seems a little sad. I reach over and press my lips to his, and he responds with accuracy. He knows how to touch me.

My body, unused to these sensations, hums with excitement.

"Will you show me what it feels like to go all the

way?"

He stares at me for the longest time, "I would like to."

"When can we do it?" I ask.

"Whenever you're ready," he replies.

"Are you kidding? I want this so much, and I'm very much overdue now."

"There's no rush. How about I take you out tomorrow?"

I notice the time and gasp.

"I forgot it was Sunday. Sorry, Markus, I have a strict routine during the week. I'm usually in bed by eight, but I'm free on Friday."

Markus stands, and my cheeks are hot as I avert my eyes from the bulge in his pants.

"You didn't drink your tea!" I exclaim, and he takes the cup and drinks it in one go.

"Ugh, cold tea. That must taste horrible."

He excuses himself, and I rush to my spare room,

Choosing Me

rummaging in my closet for my daily outfits. I set them out and select shoes to match.

I sense he is near, and when I glance over , he is standing at the door.

"Is that what you're wearing tomorrow?"

"Yes."

"Can I really not see you until Friday?"

"I do all my chores during the week. I have my hair done on Thursdays, so Friday night it is."

"Friday night is perfect."

I walk over to him, and he pulls me in for a kiss. My knees are weak.

"Good night, Dylan."

"See you on Friday."

D S Johnson - Mills

The First Cut

Toby and I sit at our lunch table, catching up. He has brought plantains from yesterday's market. That is about the extent of our craziness when we're at the office.

"D, what did you get up to yesterday?"

"Not much, as always."

"We need to find you a hobby."

If only he knew.

With a stroke of luck, Toby is called out to the

Choosing Me

Munich office and flies out on Friday morning.

He's very apologetic when we meet for lunch on Thursday and suggests I ask Markus if he is free to accompany me to the market on Sunday.

"You need to grow your circle, D."

"I'll get on that, pronto."

Friday arrives, and I dress in my new strapless jumpsuit meticulously. I add a smart jacket and scarf for the day, which I'll remove in the evening.

As soon as my day is over, I head to the ladies' room to finish my look. I apply eyeliner and mascara and touch up my lips, adding a pink leather belt around my waist. I grab my leather jacket and leave my work suit with the scarf over the back of my chair. Markus texts me that he is outside, and so, heart in hand, I head downstairs to start my weekend.

He pulls up right outside my building. I open the car door and slip in.

"You look very beautiful."

"Hi Markus," I'm suddenly feeling shy.

He is wearing a crisp white shirt and dark jeans. I thought I had his face etched in my memory, but he looks even better than I remember.

He smells good too.

I quickly buckle my seat belt. He gives me a quick kiss on the lips and starts the car engine. He tells me he's booked a table for us to have dinner, but we don't have to be there for an hour or so. He is taking me back to his place.

He pulls up to the security gates and presses a small black fob. The gates open slowly. He manoeuvres the car into a parking bay and turns off the engine.

Fear has me paralysed, and my body refuses to budge.

Clearly, I did not think this through.

He opens my door, and when I don't move, he offers me his hand. I reach out and take it nervously, then adjust my outfit and smooth my hair. We walk over to the building entrance, and he greets the man behind the security desk, who gives me a look of scrutiny. My legs turn to rubber, and I can barely take another step.

Markus leads me forward. As we wait for the lift, a couple steps out, holding hands. They stare at me, so Markus says hello. I feel like I have a scarlet S branded on my forehead. The lift is waiting, but I don't move. Markus gently pulls me inside.

He presses the green button with PH written in bold white letters. When the lift door opens, he leads me to another door on the left. He slides a key card into the lock, opens it, and we step into the most amazing apartment.

The interior is flooded with light from the fading evening. I have the sensation of stepping into the clouds. The glass walls showcase a spectacular view over the river Thames.

He places his keys into a small bowl on the counter. My heart races.

"Would you like a tour?"

"Markus, I don't like this."

"What's wrong?"

He finally catches on to my mood, taking my hand. I'm surprised that it's not obvious why I wouldn't want to come here. Butterflies flood my stomach, threatening to make me nauseous, and for the first time, I want to change my mind about this whole thing.

"Is this the home you share with her?"

"Dylan, no, of course not. This is *my* place. I moved here a few weeks ago. There's no one else here. Just us."

"Why didn't you say that before? I was so nervous."

"I'm sorry. Would you like a drink?"

"Yes, please, some water," my throat is dry, and I try to still my racing heart.

He walks over to the kitchen area, and my eyes glance around the apartment.

"I'm renting this place for a year."

"Where do you normally live?"

"Well, I've lived in Spain for the past eighteen months, but I lived with her in Fulham when I was in London. We have a house there. It's close to her gallery."

"Gallery?"

"Art Gallery. She co-owns it with her business partner."

He's standing at his breakfast bar with his hands in his pockets, leaning against the marble countertop.

"She moved to Paris in January."

"Is she coming back?"

He seems a bit reluctant, but he answers my question, "She plans to be back in the UK by late Autumn."

His pause is pregnant before he continues, "Dylan, if this makes you uncomfortable, then we don't have to..."

"I still want to, Markus, just not here."

"I'll be back in a minute," he passes me the water and goes up the stairs.

I stare out at the terrific view. A small ship floats slowly down the Thames, and I watch until it disappears. He comes down the stairs carrying a large duffle bag.

He removes cereal bars from the cupboard in the kitchen and puts them into his bag.

"Are you hungry?" he asks.

"Famished."

He takes my hand, and we leave his luxury apartment in the sky to head out into the night.

We walk to a trendy restaurant close to his place. The food is good. I have grilled fish with a salad, although Markus is not so lucky with his meal. It's quite painful to listen to his conversation with the waiter. There are only vegetarian options on the menu, even though they claim to cater to vegans.

In the end, they make him pasta with roasted vegetables. The dish swims in olive oil, but it looks delicious. To compensate, they make him a fruit salad on the house. Markus takes it all in good spirits. Clearly, hunger does not make him angry.

Choosing Me

We walk, hand in hand, back to the car. He opens the boot and removes the cereal bars from his bag, devouring them quickly while I watch. After, he discards the wrappers in a nearby bin.

He holds open the car door, I slide in, and we're off. We are both quiet on the drive. He pulls into my parking spot after what seems like ages. He switches off the engine and comes around to open my door.

I ease out of the car slowly, and he reaches out, pulling me in, kissing me until I go weak at the knees.

What is this man doing to me?

He lifts the bag from his boot, and we make our way upstairs.

As soon as we're inside, he kisses me again. He trails kisses down my neck to my chest. My breasts spill over the top of my jumpsuit. I remove my jacket, and he groans at the sight of my cleavage.

"You're beyond sexy," he whispers.

My heart rate goes into overdrive. I can't think straight.

We go to my bedroom. Removing my belt, I unzip my jumpsuit, and it falls to the ground. I step out of it, pick it up, and put it over my chair.

My hair is pinned up, and I decide to leave it. I keep my heels on and watch as he slowly removes his clothes. It's the first time I've seen him without a shirt, and I run my handover his chest, which is completely devoid of any hair.

He removes his jeans, and I put them neatly on my chair next to my jumpsuit. He smiles at me.

"Teamwork," my voice sounds husky.

He excuses himself to wash. While he's gone, I fumble for my cotton pyjamas, wishing I had something sexier. He makes me wait, and my nerves return. I sit on the edge of the armchair, shivering, but the room is warm.

When he's finished, I go into the bathroom quickly, not making eye contact.

I take longer than I need to. My eyes widen as I stare at my reflection in the mirror.

Choosing Me

"What're you doing?" I whisper to myself, but I have no answer to that question.

The build-up to this moment has perhaps blinded my better judgement. I am not an impulsive person. I'm not this girl who makes foolish decisions or sleeps with men I've only just met.

I sit on the edge of the bathtub, trying to still my racing heart, but I can't feel my legs. The seconds turn into minutes until the soft ping of the clock in my kitchen indicates an hour has passed. I stand and go to him. I walk in with my bathrobe wrapped around me.

He sits on the bed. He wears only his briefs, and I stare at his body, mesmerised by his beauty. I run my hands down his torso. He has lean muscles everywhere, and his abdominal muscles are rock solid. Finding my courage, I remove my robe, and he exhales.

"Beautiful...," he whispers.

He reaches his hand up to caress my face. His fingertips are cool against my overheated skin. I close my eyes; his touch dispels my fears. His lips press against mine, and my mouth opens.

His mouth tastes minty fresh. Our tongues touch, and I wrap my arms around him.

I want this.

He pulls me down on top of him and rolls me gently onto my back. His rock-hard erection presses against my soft stomach, and my body freezes.

He kisses me again and moans, moving to my breasts, kissing my hardened nipples.

My body melts from every touch, every kiss. The cold feeling from earlier is a distant memory.

"Markus?"

He stops and gazes into my eyes, "Yes?"

He can probably feel my racing heart.

"I'm terrified."

"Do you want me to stop?"

I shake my head, "No."

I lick my lips and press them against his, once,

twice, and again. I enjoy kissing his lips very much.

He returns my kisses with more urgency. His hands are warm now, and he caresses my body, touching me everywhere - my breasts, hips, tummy, and core - I cry out.

"You're ready," he whispers.

I watch as he puts the condom on, and I gasp at the size of him.

"Markus, I'm scared," my voice comes out strangled, and I'm shaking so hard the bed vibrates.

"It's okay," he soothes, "I'll be gentle."

He runs his hand down my tummy and between my legs. I reach for him, and he pulls me into his arms.

"Relax."

He positions between my legs and pushes into me, easing slowly. I tense my muscles, and he stops.

"Don't stop," I say, excited to finally have this experience.

He pushes against my entrance, and I think *he*

won't fit.

I'm not sure what is more dominant, the fear or the excitement. I suspect both are in equal measure.

"Dylan, try to relax," he caresses my inner thighs.

I release my held breath; the smell of my arousal is potent. I taste it on my tongue. He moves deeper. The pressure builds, and my intimate muscles open.

I look down at our bodies joining. The vision of him between my legs, sinking slowly into my body, is unreal. He eases in more, and my fingers grip tighter. He stops.

"You, okay?" he asks, closing his eyes and pressing his forehead to mine.

"Mmm..."

Our lips touch softly, gently. I open, savouring his sweetness. He moans into my mouth. I pull him closer, and he eases in more.

He bares his full weight, and his arms tremble slightly.

I pull him down onto my chest, crying out from

the hot pain. He stops and waits for a while. He kisses my forehead and my eyes, slowly moving to my lips, deepening the kiss. He starts to move again.

My muscles strain, and I don't think I can take much more. I want to beg him to stop so I can take a break, but he wraps me closer in his arms and closes his eyes. He whispers my name.

Warmth flows through my body. Instinctively, I push against him, ignoring the pain. He opens his eyes and smiles at me.

"You feel exquisite," he whispers, his voice breaking.

I pull his face closer, press my lips against his and tentatively touch his tongue with mine.

His breathing accelerates, and he starts to move inside me, very slowly at first, then increasing the pace ever so slightly. I move my hips trying to keep up with him, and he gazes into my eyes.

The end comes too soon. After a few minutes, he gently pulls out of me. Cold air replaces his warmth, and my fingers grasp the empty sheets.

"Markus?"

"I'm here," his voice is close.

He lifts me in his arms, and I cling to him. He prepares a bath. The water is hot and soothes my bruised muscles. I sigh and lay back, closing my eyes. He uses a washcloth and cleans me gently.

"Do you mind if I come in with you?"

I open my eyes, "No, I don't mind."

He climbs in behind me. I nestle between his legs, with my head on his chest.

"How do you feel?" his voice sounds far away.

"Good. Really shattered," I say as my eyes drift, "Why is that?" I ask.

"It happens sometimes after sex. You've used up a lot of energy," he kisses my hair, "Come on, I'll put you to bed."

He climbs out of the bath.

"Where do you keep your bed linen?"

My eyes open briefly. I was not expecting this

question.

"The cupboard in the spare bedroom."

"Relax," he bends and softly kisses my lips, "I'll be back shortly."

I almost fall asleep in the bath. He comes back with a large towel. He helps me stand, wrapping the towel around my body. The sheets have been changed.

Is this guy for real?

He lies on my side of the bed, gazing at me, and I stand at the foot of the bed, looking at him.

"What?"

I walk round to the other side of the bed.

"I usually sleep there."

I climb in. He lifts me and changes sides, laughing softly. His eyes are shining and wide awake just before I fall away.

Falling in Deep

The sunlight threatens to burst through my blinds. I sit up, wincing from the tight and sore sensation between my legs. Markus sleeps peacefully. His face is relaxed. Leaning over, I gently press my lips to his, and he smiles.

"Good morning, beautiful," he whispers.

"Hey," I reply shyly.

"Sleep, okay?"

"Yes. I'm sorry about last night, about after...I

couldn't seem to stay awake."

"Last night was about you."

"I wanted it to be good for you too."

"It was," he pulls me into his arms, "Sex isn't the same every time. I had to be gentle. It meant having to stop when I wanted to carry on. I didn't want to hurt you."

I hang on to his every word, feeling reassured. My tummy rumbles at that moment.

"Breakfast?" I ask, as I'm famished.

"I'll shower first," he says, kissing my lips.

Breakfast is homemade granola with maple syrup. I'd researched what to feed vegans, and it's not as complicated as I thought. With the mix ready and in the oven, I set the table and open the windows to let more sunlight into my lounge.

His apartment is spacious compared to my tiny one.

I hope he does not become claustrophobic when he's here.

My place is perfect for me; I love it. I think about his ex, whoever she is, and wonder how someone could be unhappy when they could live in a place like that.

"Smells amazing in here," he says.

He's dressed in jeans and a dark brown polo shirt. It makes his green eyes pop. Removing the bowl from the oven, I dish up, slicing a banana and adding it to the mix.

"It's ready."

After placing the jug with the warm coconut milk in the middle, I wait for him to sit on the chair facing the kitchen. I sit across from him and dig in.

"This is very good. You made this?"

"Yes. Its organic oats mixed with rapeseed oil, maple syrup, and pumpkin seeds, tossed and baked in the oven for twenty minutes."

"Granola from a box will never be the same again."

"It must be a bummer when restaurants don't

cater to you."

"I wanted to take you somewhere nice. That restaurant is new, and the reviews were good. They'll eventually catch on," he says between bites, "I have a few places I eat at regularly, so I'm usually well-fed."

"What would you like to do today?" he asks.

"I'm not sure,"

I wonder if it's too soon for more sex,

"Whatever you want."

"What would you be doing today if I weren't here?"

"Cleaning, cooking, boring stuff."

"Well, I don't clean, and I don't cook."

"Your place looked spotless. Who cleans it?"

"I have a cleaner."

"And a cook too?"

"No. I mostly eat out."

"Every day?"

"Yes, but sometimes I order food in."

"But you made the bed last night."

"I *can* do it. I just don't."

"Well, there's no time like the present to start doing it again. I'm going to shower so you can do the dishes."

I dress in jeans and a maroon cotton sweater. When I join him in the lounge, the dishes have been washed and put away. He is sitting at my table, texting on his phone. I walk in, and his face lights up when he sees me. He pulls me onto his lap and kisses me.

"You look lovely."

He touches my hair, still wrapped in its pins, "I like your hair like this."

He touches my face, kisses my eyes and my lips.

"Do you wear Makeup?"

"No. Do I look too plain?"

"Not in the slightest. You really are a beautiful woman."

"I have an idea about what we can do today if

you're up for it..." he says, suddenly grinning like a schoolboy, "It's not too far from here."

A few minutes later, we're driving through winding country lanes, finally pulling into a deserted place called an underground bunker.

"Have you brought me out here to murder me?"

"No, it's an outdoor paintballing arena. I used to come here in secondary school, but it's been ages."

"Paintballing? I can't play these games. Whenever I'm in these types of situations, I become completely feral."

"I'd love to do this with you," he says, smiling.

How can I resist this face?

"Okay, I'm in, but don't say I didn't warn you."

* * *

By the time we are heading home, I'm starving. Markus suggests we go to a restaurant for dinner as we skipped lunch. I tell him I'll cook him something at my place, and his eyes light up.

I saw another side to him today during our

gruelling four-hour paintballing session. We had to team up with another group of people, and by the end of the first session, they all loved him. He's very likeable. It must be his ability to remain cool and calm; attributes that I don't possess. He made friends, and I made enemies.

Back at my place, he asks me to take a shower with him, but I decline, telling him I don't think sex in the bathroom is very hygienic. He is amused, chuckling as he goes in on his own. He's singing in the shower, and he sounds sweet. I put on music and head to the kitchen to start making dinner.

I'm making a vegan lasagne, and I have all the ingredients ready. The dish is quite simple, but I appreciate how it will not taste the same without cheese. To compensate, I add extra garlic to the white sauce.

When Markus leaves the bathroom, I decide to shower while the lasagne is in the oven, asking him to listen out for the timer. I take my time washing every part of me. My body feels different. I'm rubbing the moisturiser into my skin when he comes to the door.

Choosing Me

I'm completely naked.

"Did the timer go off?"

"Yes, a few minutes ago."

Rushing into the kitchen, I switch off the oven. When I return to my room, he is sitting on my chair.

Feeling brave, I walk over to him. He kisses between my thighs and caresses my fleshy bottom. I'm instantly aroused, and my heart rate spikes. I like what he is doing.

"Are you still sore?"

"No, it feels a bit better than it did this morning."

He stands up. I lower my eyes, suddenly feeling shy. He gently lifts my head, gazing into my eyes. My lips part slightly, and he bends to kiss me softly. I mould my body to his and run my hands through his soft hair. He palms my bottom, lifting me off the ground.

He breaks the kiss, and I pant as he lays me on the bed. He breathes heavily, and I watch as he opens a condom and slips it on. I close my eyes as he urges me to open for him. He pushes my legs wider and slowly eases into me.

I wince as my tight flesh gives way to his touch.

"Dylan," he whispers, "Exquisite," he pauses.

His eyes are pools of dark desire. He swears softly and penetrates me deeper. His weight presses into me, and I revel in the sensations. My mouth opens slightly as I try to absorb these intense sensations that are all new to me.

Trying to match his velocity, I soon give up as I've not been here before. I can only lie under him, squirming with pleasure as he consumes me.

He thrusts inside my body over and over, and waves of ecstasy wash over me.

"Markus!" I cry out.

His mouth crashes onto mine, and he sucks on my lips and neck, moving deeper into my overheated centre, driving me wild.

"Come for me, Dylan."

Like an obedient girl, I bow to his request and let

go, falling down the precipice of ecstasy. My body trembles violently from the impact, but he holds me as he, too, releases with my name on his lips. He removes the condom and discards it before coming back to bed and pulling me into his arms.

"Are you alright?"

I nod. It's all I can manage at this moment. He kisses my forehead, and I feel myself drifting.

When I come to, cocooned in his arms, the light from the window has faded to a dull pink hue. His hand is on my shoulder, caressing my skin. It feels easy, natural, to lie here with him in this way, as if we belong to each other.

I sit up to move out of his embrace and wince; my body is bruised and battered. His hand goes to my hair which has come loose. He sits up behind me and trails kisses down my naked back.

His erection presses against my bum, and I turn to look at his naked body.

Instinctively, I reach my finger out to touch him. His phallus is rock hard, but the tip is soft.

"What does It feel like without a condom?"

"Skin to skin is the best feeling."

"Really? Can we try it?"

He looks at me for a while but does not speak.

"What?"

"I'd like very much to feel you, but I wasn't sure you'd be okay with that."

"Yes, I want to. Show me everything."

His fingers brush against my core.

"You're wet," he whispers, his eyes flushed with desire.

The sheet conceals my lower half, so he moves his hand under, slipping his finger inside; I bite my lower lip. His eyes are on my face, and I can't seem to tear my gaze away from his.

He kneels and positions between my thighs, which are slick with juices from my body. The heady smell permeates my senses. When he removes his finger, he brings it to his lips, tasting me. My eyes go wide. He offers it to me, and I suck the salty taste off his finger. He groans loudly and sinks into my slippery centre. He is warmer and the sweetness is magnified. He swears softly.

When he moves inside me this time, I feel so much more of him. I'm not sure where the sensation starts. The pleasure is blinding as the pressure builds instantly.

"You're so beautiful," he whispers.

Tears pool in his eyes. He is the first man to take me all the way, but I somehow know his reaction is not normal. His emotions pour into every thrust. I throw my head back and moan loudly.

Suddenly, he stops and pulls out of me. Tears come to my eyes.

"What's wrong?"

"Sorry, I almost came inside of you," he's on his back, breathing hard.

"Oh."

"When did you last menstruate?"

"Ugh, don't remind me. It's due any day now."

"Are you sure?"

"I can always tell; my breasts are larger, and I am fatter and moody."

He kisses me again with more urgency, and I forget my name. He sucks on my nipples one by one until I cry out. The feeling is unbelievable.

He rolls me onto my back and enters me again, pushing slowly. I'm saturated but stay with him, riding this wave of pleasure. He takes me to the deepest depths of desire, guiding me, and foolishly, I follow.

"I'll come inside of you," he whispers against my lips.

"Yes," I say as his seed fills me.

"Dylan..."

He pulls out and lies on his back, easing me on top of him, kissing my face and running his thumb over my lips.

"What are you doing to me?" he whispers.

I'm pleased with myself. He dozes off, and I take the chance to observe him.

Choosing Me

He looks so young lying here.

I run my hand over the contours of his face, down to his chest and his tummy. I lean over and trail kisses all over his torso. His hand rubs my back and moves up to my hair. It's messy again, but I decide to leave it. He opens his eyes.

I kiss him on his mouth, and he holds me and deepens the kiss.

"Are you hungry?" I ask when he comes up for air.

"Yes," he whispers, but I know he is not talking about food.

He moves into a sitting position, pulling me onto his lap. He closes his eyes. His fingers lightly brush against my core, and I gasp. I'm drenched from our mingled juices. He lifts me and slides me onto his erection, and suddenly, I'm terrified.

"Markus, I don't know how to do it this way."

"Just move with me."

His hands are on my hips. I try to move slowly at

first, but my confidence wanes. He pushes me backwards. I wobble slightly, and he palms my waist.

"I've got you."

This position is more intimate. The sweet sensations spread from my core to my belly, heating me up. We move in perfect unison. His hands are on my thighs as he watches me. He smiles wondrously as I come alive.

"Markus."

My body soars to dizzying heights. My orgasm is quick but strong. I sag against him as my energy seeps from every orifice. He goes rigid before his body relaxes as he releases again, and we lay together panting.

"Are you alright?" he whispers.

"Yes," I reply.

My eyelids droop as fatigue pulls me under.

Later, after we've showered, we eat the lasagne with a garden salad. Famished, I eat two slices, and Markus eats three.

Choosing Me

I open a bottle of Merlot, and he is impressed. I can't take all the credit, so I tell him this is Toby's favourite.

I offer him a box of vegan chocolates. He tries to feed me one, but I decline, telling him that I'm sweet enough. He grabs me and pulls me onto his lap.

"That's so true," he replies.

I prepare for bed much later that evening, and Markus lies down on the fresh sheets watching me. I'm searching for alternative night attire besides my cotton ones.

"I don't have anything sexy to wear to bed."

Thoroughly spent, I pull on a fresh pair of cotton pyjamas and crawl in beside him. He pulls me closer, and we lie facing each other.

"I can take you shopping tomorrow if you like. I'd love to see you in silk," he says, running his hands down my hip.

I stare at his hand as it moves and I frown,

"Markus, I'm not expecting that."

I don't want to be like a kept woman. I want to stay in control of this, whatever this is.

"In fact, it's probably best if we just keep things more casual," I say.

"Is that what you want?"

"Yes, I think it would be better that way. I don't want to over-complicate things."

He stares at me, but I can't read his face. I've given up trying to figure out what he is thinking, so I smile just to try something. He smiles in return, kisses me on the forehead, and pulls me into his arms.

I drift into a sea of warmth.

* * *

All too soon, he is shaking me awake.

"Dylan? You're bleeding."

I recognise the familiar cramps.

"Speak of the devil. The evil curse has arrived."

The bleeding is heavier than normal, and his pyjamas are soiled. I roll out of bed slowly, apologising for the blood on his clothes.

He helps me to clean up and change my sheets. I shower and make breakfast, but I'm bloated, and it's making me miserable as I was hoping we could have more sex. We sit to eat oatmeal and don't say much to each other.

"I'll do the dishes," he offers.

He clears the table, and I'm grateful. I sit on my couch, wanting to put my feet up today and not do much. Markus offers me tea and sits with me while I drink it. He pulls me onto his lap and rests my head on his chest. His fingers caress my hair.

His affectionate behaviour makes me a little nervous, but it feels wonderful, so I don't object. My cramps are hurting more than normal.

"Are you in pain?" he rubs my tummy, but I'm self-conscious as it's quite swollen.

In fact, every part of my anatomy seems to have doubled in size. It's such poor timing.

"Yes," I say, and then sigh.

"Do you want me to make you feel better?"

"Can you make my cramps go away?"

"I have a tried and tested remedy."

I sit up and scrutinize his face. He is giving me that blazing look again. He lifts me off his lap and takes my hand.

"Go and shower," he says, and I do as I am told.

I come back to my room wrapped in my towel, and he has spread clean towels on my bed. He removes the one I have around me. He is already naked, and the sight of him exposed in my room arouses me.

This is a surprise, as I never feel sexy during my period. He takes my hand and sits me on the bed, making sure I am on the towels.

"Lie back," he says.

I'm at the foot of my bed, and my feet are touching the floor.

He runs his hands over my tummy. My breasts are swollen and throbbing painfully. I want him to kiss them. My upper back lifts slightly, anticipating his warm mouth on my nipples, but he doesn't do it. He looks at my body, bends, and runs his tongue from my navel to my core. I whimper.

He lifts my leg, entering me hard. I cry out. My core is slick from the blood and my arousal, and he slides inside me with much more ease than before.

"Does this feel okay?"

"Mm... it's good."

It only takes three swift strokes before my body convulses. I gasp in surprise as I release almost immediately. He follows soon after, spilling inside of me. He pulls out of me just as quickly, his shaft glistening from our intermingled fluids.

"Don't move. I'll be right back."

When he returns, he pulls me into his embrace, wrapping the towels around my lower body. The cramps have stopped.

"How did you do that?"

"Do you feel better?"

"I do, thank you."

"Trade secret," he whispers and palms my stomach.

"I didn't think you could have sex during periods," I speak cautiously, not wanting to appear too naïve about sexual exploits.

"Sure, you can. You just did."

"I feel like such a rookie with you."

"It comes with experience. The important thing is to know what you like and don't like."

He drops feather-light kisses on my shoulder.

"I like everything you do to me," I whisper.

"What's your favourite thing to do when you're having sex?" I ask.

"I'm not sure it works like that. For me, sex is about giving pleasure, so it always depends on what my partner responds to."

I'm fixated on every word he speaks, "How do you know what I like?"

Choosing Me

"It's easy with you. I see it on your face. I know when it's too much or just what you can handle. You're a very sensual woman. You absorb everything. I barely touch you, and you are so ready. I don't know...maybe it's because this is all new for you."

His fingers lightly caress my arm, causing goosebumps to rise.

"I don't think so. I think it's you and your skills."

I melt as soon as he touches me.

"I've never felt like this. I want you to teach me everything you know. I would love to be a goddess in the bedroom."

"You already are."

I think about his words as I clean myself in the shower. He is lying on his back with his eyes closed when I return. I sit on the edge of the bed, reaching my hand to touch the muscles of his stomach.

"Markus, can I ask you something?"

He opens his eyes and turns to his side. His hand is on my thigh, "Anything."

"You stayed hard."

"It would've been difficult not to. You are hmm..."

I have never considered that I could be desirable, but I had good reason.

"How old were you? When you got engaged?"

"Eighteen. I've known him most of my life. Everyone assumed we were a couple before I knew it myself. He was the captain of the football team, and I was the head cheerleader. Homecoming King and Queen. I guess we were caught up in the high school romance. He proposed in front of the entire auditorium, and I just said yes."

"We went away to Yale together, but then, it was different. No one knew who we were. No one cared, thank goodness. We tried to have sex a few times, but he would always lose his erection," I pause as the emotions come back to me, "I was confused, but we didn't talk about it much. Then he had sex with someone else, probably to ensure it worked."

I laugh, but Markus is intent on every word.

"She had such pleasure in telling me. He was mortified, and I felt sorry for him, but I wasn't mad, so I gave him back his ring."

"Perhaps you weren't ready. Love and sex are not mutually exclusive."

"I suppose you are right. Thank you for making my first time so incredible."

"You're welcome."

* * *

Toby calls late in the afternoon. I sit on my bed in the spare bedroom, catching up with my buddy.

"How is my favourite diva?"

"Missing her best bud like crazy."

"Did you go to the market with Markus?"

"I have my menses."

"TMI D. No need to overshare."

"Are you in the office tomorrow?"

"No, they've asked me to stay on. The revenue services have been investigating."

"What?"

"I'll stay until the audit is complete and then do some recruiting."

"I didn't hear about this?"

"You'll probably hear about it tomorrow. It was all very last minute."

I don't speak for a while, and he interprets my silence to mean something else.

"I can arrange for you to come to the Munich office to work," he offers.

"No, it's fine, Toby. I'm a big girl."

"I worry about you being alone. Do you mind if I ask Markus to check in on you?"

"Yes, sure," I say, grinning to myself.

* * *

"Toby is staying in Munich for a while. He's planning on asking you to keep me company," I say while we have dinner.

"I can pick you up, and we can have lunch if you

like."

"I'd like that."

"It's the downside of having only one friend in this great big city."

"Why don't you have more people in your life?"

"People always somehow disappoint," I say, shrugging my shoulders.

He reaches out and takes my hand, "You're here on your own, and you have no family around you."

"This is by design. I don't feel like I'm missing out. I have Toby."

He gazes at me, playing with my fingers before bringing them to his lips, "It's almost your bedtime."

"I do feel strangely tired."

"I can tuck you in if you like."

"No. I can manage."

"Dylan, this weekend with you was very special. Thank you."

"For me too."

I walk with him to the spare room and watch as he packs his bag. I act on the impulse of the moment.

"You can leave some clothes for when you stay over again."

His eyes hold mine for a moment too long, and after a while, I look away, folding my arms. We did not discuss whether our weekend together was a one-off. I don't want to make any assumptions, but one weekend is not enough.

Choosing Me

Happy

As I walk to the office on Monday, I am unable to remove the grin from my face. I've finally been let in on a secret the whole world knows about. I spend the morning blissfully happy even though I'm wearing my bloated day pants.

The rumour mill has gone into overdrive about the investigation at the head office in Munich, but I don't let on that I already know.

Markus and I meet up outside my office building.

He carries a small square plastic bag with a handle

and greets me with a kiss, reaching for my hand as we cross the street.

"What's that?"

"It's a blanket. How was your morning?"

"It's been quite busy," I reply.

He opens the gate and gestures for me to go first. The day is pleasant and warm in the sunshine. The park is packed with a lunchtime crowd. We find a little secluded space, and Markus spreads his blanket.

I remove my backpack, jacket, and shoes, and sit. I give Markus his lunch and start digging into mine, as I must ensure I'm back at my desk on time. I made him a black quinoa salad with olives and sundried tomatoes.

"Dylan, this is delicious. Where did you learn to make food like this?"

"My grandmother."

"Is she back home?"

His eyes are bright green in the sunshine.

"She died not too long ago."

Choosing Me

"I'm sorry."

We are both silent for a while.

"Sometimes, I miss her so much, the pain is unreal, but I suppose it's only natural to feel that way. She helped daddy to raise us."

"What about your mother?"

"She wasn't well, and our dad worked on the road. It wasn't easy with two young girls, so my sister and I lived with our grandparents."

He stares at me with pity in his eyes, and this annoys me. I wish he would stop asking me these questions. It's so typical, English, and middle-class.

He probably thinks everyone has the same life as he does.

"Are you finished?"

I start packing up, not waiting for his answer. He senses the shift in my mood and tries to hold my hand, but I pull away.

"I don't mean to pry. Forgive me."

"I'm not looking for your sympathy. My life is not

like yours, perfect, with your mommy and daddy, who you can visit every other Sunday for brunch."

"Actually, I'm hoping I can spend my Sundays with you."

He brushes a stray strand of my hair behind my ear, and I stop to stare at him. He scoots over closer to me and runs his hand along my top. His lips brush lightly against mine, and I forget my annoyance.

"What are your plans for this evening?" he asks politely.

It breaks my resolve, and I kiss him back with fervour. He breaks the kiss too soon, and it's a moment before I can answer.

"I'm going home after work. I always chill, put my feet up, watch TV or read a book when I'm on my monthlies."

I run my fingers down his silk tie. His clothes must be expensive. I glance down at my H&M trousers; they're very trendy but seem cheap next to his Austin Reed-type suit.

Choosing Me

Is that how we look together?

"If you like, I can take you home after work. I won't stay if you prefer."

He sounds so formal and upper-crust.

"Sure, I'd like that. I better head back."

I try to stand, and he helps me up. He is always so kind and polite, and I'm slightly repentant for snapping at him.

It's funny how I'm never annoyed when we're in bed. Maybe because sex is the only reason we are together, and I shouldn't forget it.

He walks me back to my building and kisses me goodbye, "See you later. I'll be here at four."

I spend the rest of the day thinking about him and his complication. He is calm, cool, and always collected, so it makes me wonder what the issue is with him and her. I don't know her name, and I don't plan to ask. There must be more to him than he lets on. No one can be that smooth.

True to his word, he picks me up in his car and

drives me home. Once we are inside my apartment door, he pulls me into his arms and kisses me. I haven't removed my bag from my shoulder. He holds me captive with my back against the door, his tongue explores mine, and his fingers pinch my sensitive nipples. I moan softly. He stops, releases me, and smiles.

"I've wanted to do that since lunchtime," he says.

My heart rate has spiked. Honestly, being with him sends my heart into constant overdrive. I look on the bright side, thinking of all the calories I must be burning.

After showering, I dress in cotton shorts and put on a sleeveless croptop that exposes my tummy.

When I join him in the lounge, I notice that he has removed his work clothes and is wearing jeans and a grey polo shirt. He is always well-groomed. I want to change my outfit, but he tells me I look sexy, so I decide not to bother. Dinner tonight is yesterday's leftovers.

A little while later, Markus helps me to dry the

dishes and put them away. He appears to be over his initial shock after discovering I don't own a dishwasher.

"I have tickets to a party on Saturday. I'd like you to accompany me," he says.

"What kind of party?"

"A semi-formal gathering."

"I don't have anything suitable to wear."

"The party is on a river boat. You're only required to dress warmly. It will be cold."

"Who else will be there?"

I am not sure I like this at all.

I don't want to meet his upper-crust friends.

"I don't know who else has bought tickets."

He turns to look at me. My hair has come loose, and he tucks it behind my ear.

"Why not?" I say, and his face lights up.

Toby calls at seven; he is still at the office. I wonder if I should tell him that Markus is here, but I decide not to. I sit on my couch with the blanket over my legs.

"I'll be home this weekend. I'm coming to see my girl."

"I can't wait. I'll plan something for us to do."

Markus is looking at an old photo album when I hang up.

"Is this you?"

"Yes."

"How old are you in this picture?"

"Thirteen, I think."

I remember the day it was taken. We were on a picnic at Boston Common. I don't remember who took the photo; I think maybe it was Sam. I curl up under the blanket, happy and relaxed after talking with Toby.

He questions me about the photographs, "Who is this?"

"My grandmother. This picture is the oldest one in the album. It was taken on her wedding day."

Choosing Me

"The resemblance between you two is uncanny; she's beautiful."

"Yes, she was."

Tears fall down my face, and he pulls me into his arms. Losing Grams was tough. I used to have that picture on my bedside table, but I couldn't look at it anymore after she died.

"Thank you," says Markus.

"For what?" I rest my head on his chest.

He smells good.

"You don't like to talk about your family, but I was curious. Hope that's okay?" he brushes my hair back from my face.

"It's hard to talk about them; I miss her every day. It hasn't been long since she died. She was my guiding light, and I felt lost for a while until I met Toby. She sent him to me; he helps."

We are both quiet for a while. His attention is too intimate, so I pull away from his embrace, moving to the farthest point on the couch.

"I better go now."

I move to stand, but he tells me to stay where I am.

"You look comfy," he dips his head and kisses me softly on the lips.

"See you tomorrow," he says.

I hear him close the front door, and I breathe out. I didn't realise that I was holding my breath.

* * *

Markus and I are sitting in the small park again today. We have just finished lunch.

"I have a prior engagement tonight, but I can arrange for you to be driven home if you like."

"Markus, I know how to make my way home by now but thank you."

"Sorry, I guess it's become a habit," he replies.

He is lying back on his elbows, gazing at me. It's another sunny day, and the light is reflecting in his eyes. They're light green today. He's removed his tie and rolled up his shirt sleeves.

Choosing Me

He's effortlessly gorgeous.

"What's a habit?" I lean over to kiss him quickly on his lips.

He grabs me, prolonging the kiss. When he releases me, I'm breathless. I glance over my shoulder to see if anyone in the park has noticed, but no one is looking at us.

"Wanting to take care of you, it's become a bit of a habit of mine. Wanting to kiss you as well. I could do that all day," he brushes his thumb over my lips.

"You're a very good kisser," I say.

"She obviously taught you well," I whisper under my breath.

He sits up suddenly, startling me, his eyes blazing, "If you want to ask me about her, you can."

"I'm not curious about her," I say too quickly.

He trails kisses down my neck. I'm wearing a pink blouse with buttons down the front. He runs his fingers along my collarbone, so I close my eyes and enjoy the sensations.

"Thank you for lunch and dessert," he whispers, his lips touching mine.

I want to tell him this kind of kissing is extra, but I'm speechless. He stands and offers me his hand, pulling me up. We pack up. He stops outside my building and kisses me.

Oh well, I might as well enjoy these kisses while I can.

* * *

I notice his message the next morning. He wants to take me to a restaurant for lunch. I am flustered trying to figure out what to wear. I've tried on several different outfits, none of which felt right. Finally, I settle on the original one I had picked out on Sunday. I'm late for work, so I don't have time to do my hair, and by the time lunch comes around, I'm already in a bad mood.

I grab my jacket and bag and walk downstairs. He's waiting outside my building, dapper in his work suit and wearing his usual smile.

"Hi."

Choosing Me

"Hey," I reply, "Where are we going?"

I can't shake this negative feeling. I am curious about what he did after work yesterday evening, but I don't want to admit that. It doesn't help that he's shown up looking happy and relaxed.

I hope we're not going to one of his vegan restaurants.

He hails a taxi and holds the door for me to climb in. My sour mood doesn't seem to faze him.

"How was your morning?"

"Busy," I shrug.

"You look beautiful," he says.

I glare at him as if he is nuts but thank him for his compliment.

The cabbie pulls over at a riverside restaurant. There is a busy lunchtime crowd. A tall guy with dreads comes over, greeting Markus warmly.

"Nate, thank you for doing this."

He introduces me, and I smile politely, taking his hand.

"Nate owns the restaurant and was kind enough to fit us in for lunch."

"Dylan, you're like a ray of sunshine," says Nate.

"Thanks Nate, it's nice to meet you."

He ushers us to the back and up the winding staircase to the roof. The view is stunning. It's a fine day, and we can see all the way across the Thames, overlooking CanaryWharf.

Tall palm trees and Hibiscus flowers are dotted around the rooftop space. A small table set for two stands under a canopy at the end of the roof. Nate holds my chair, and I sit. Then he gives me a menu.

"What can I get you to drink?" Nate asks.

I order my usual lemon water.

"Very good," he replies and walks away.

He returns with my lemon water and fruit juice for Markus. His drink looks divine; strawberries are floating in it, making my water look tame.

"What's that?" I ask.

"It's Nate's special version of strawberries and

cream. Try some."

"Wow, that's amazing. How do you make this?" I ask.

"Freshly creamed coconut," he replies.

"What would you like to eat?"

"Can I have whatever he's having?"

"Coming right up," he smiles warmly as he leaves us.

I take Markus' drink and try some more.

"How'd you discover this place? It's amazing."

"One of the partners at work recommended that I try it out. I come here most lunchtimes when I'm in the office. Nate, being Rastafarian, has no dairy, so he knows how to prepare my meals without any fuss."

"What are we having?"

"I think today's special is mushroom stroganoff with rice and peas."

"I'd never have imagined you coming to a Caribbean restaurant and having lunch."

"Why is that?"

"You just seem like such a well-bred city boy."

"City boys need to eat."

The way he speaks suggests that he is no longer talking about the stroganoff Caribbean style.

* * *

I'm a few minutes late going back to the office, but my mood is soaring. I enjoyed my afternoon lunch with Markus and sent him a text to thank him. The rest of my day goes by in a flash, and soon he arrives outside my building, waiting to take me home. The traffic is extremely heavy, and we've been sitting in it for a while. He is cool and calm, as usual.

"I'm having my hair done tomorrow evening."

He reaches over to my hair, smoothing it back,

"What are you having done?"

"Are you putting in a request?"

"Does it go in an afro?"

"Not really, my hair texture is a bit different. It's

soft and wavy, so I mostly have it washed and flat-ironed. I can wash it myself, but it always goes frizzy, and I hate that."

I'm looking out the window, bewildered by the traffic jam.

"I'll pick you up after if you like."

"Do you take your car every day?"

I've not walked much this week.

"Yes, mostly."

He checks his map, "I think there must be an incident up ahead. I'll try another way."

"Markus, I can just take the tube home."

"I want to spend the evening with you."

He turns the car around in the middle of the road. The traffic lights turn red. He gazes over at me, and our eyes lock for a moment. The lights change, and he starts off. My heart is hammering in my chest.

He takes a longer route to my place, and I stare out the window. The landscape is flashing by with such speed that I cannot register where we are. This is what it feels like, this whirlwind affair I find myself a part of.

Back at my place, I'm going through the motions. My mind is occupied by what happened in the car earlier.

Is he becoming too attached to me?

Guilt consumes me. I pull my dress over my head and sit on the bed.

"Dylan, everything ok?" he appears at the door.

He comes into my room and sits on my chair in the corner, looking at me, but I don't say anything.

"Hey, what's wrong?"

"I'm not sure. This doesn't feel right."

"Do you want me to go?"

My eyes finally meet his, "No, I like you being here. I just worry that you like being here too."

We both laugh.

"I know that makes no sense. I'm not impulsive, but I don't feel in control of this situation."

Choosing Me

"What is it that scares you?"

"I don't want things to become muddled. I'm not looking for anything else."

"Do you know how special you are?" he whispers.

My heart takes off like a rocket. I wonder if he hears it, sitting so close to me. He looks into my eyes, and his emerald ones are ablaze. I lean forward and kiss him, tentatively caressing his lips with the tip of my tongue.

"Mm...." I moan softly as his hand caresses my back.

"Sweet," he whispers against my lips.

I break the kiss, and his eyes hold mine. As if in a trance, I continue to stare. My head screams at me to stop this now, but my heart, beating erratically, spurs me on.

"Make love to me."

"Are you still bleeding?" his voice is barely a whisper.

"It's the fourth day. The heavy flow has stopped."

As I speak, he traces my lips with his thumb, and my breath hitches. I concede tonight, as I don't know what is happening.

Standing up from the bed, I lift my dress over my head and slowly remove my bra and panties. I am conscious of the bleeding, even though it is much reduced.

I roll my panties in my hands, suddenly embarrassed. There are spots of blood, and I want to discard my towel first.

"I just need a moment," I mumble and walk away swiftly.

I clean up with fast movements and hurry back to him.

My pulse races painfully, "Sorry about that."

He removes his shirt and pants. After bending me over on the bed so I fall on my hands, he enters me from behind. It all happens so fast; the pain brings tears to my eyes. His warm hands slide down the contours of my body.

Choosing Me

He feels so full inside. This sensation is very new, and it takes me a while to adjust. He kisses my back, reaching around to fondle my breasts, and I begin to melt.

He penetrates deeper, and a sharp pain shoots through my stomach. He says my name, and I grit my teeth and meet his thrust. My hands buckle as I have reached my limit, so he pulls out of me and turns me over onto my back.

Sliding inside my overheated centre, he wraps my legs around him. My body is slightly elevated, and he is rock-hard. It feels different this way. The pain is gone, replaced by sweet ecstasy.

"Dylan..." he moves faster.

As pleasure devours me, my moans echo in the room, "Markus...so good."

My words are incoherent as my body reaches the pinnacle. Gripping his shoulders tightly, I hold on until he lets go, releasing onto my stomach.

I reach down to touch it, but my arms have become weak and fall to my side. He cleans me as I lie comatose on the bed.

Afterwards, he lies next to me, enfolding me in his arms. My hair is wild and spilling all around me. His fingers tremble as he brushes it away from my face.

"You, okay?"

I nod and adjust myself, conscious that there might be blood on my sheets. I lie on my side, facing him.

"Did I hurt you?"

"A little."

"I'm sorry," he cuddles me closer.

"Why does it still hurt?" I ask as he caresses my arms.

"I think you just have to give it time."

"Sorry, this must be annoying for you, I did try, but it was quite painful."

"Dylan, being with you is intoxicating. I don't think you realise just how desirable you are. Since the moment I met you, it's as if I've wandered into someone else's dream."

Choosing Me

I place my palm flat on his chest, his heart beats steadily while mine goes wild. His words please me very much. I want to find some way to return the compliment and let him know that I, too, am caught up in his spell.

"Will you stay with me tonight?"

"Yes," he whispers.

Selfless

Markus has a meeting that runs over the next day, so I don't see him until he picks me up from my hairdresser after eight. Last night, he held me in his arms all evening. He suggested taking me out to dinner tonight, so I wore my black fitted pencil dress and broke out the Louboutin's.

I walk to the hairdresser in my flats. The salon is a twenty minutes' walk from my office, and I don't want to scuff my heels as they only come out on special occasions. I ask my hairdresser, Paul, to leave my natural curls.

He is in his element, as he has always wanted me to show my curls. I decided to let Markus see me with my natural hair since he seemed curious. I slip on my heels at the salon and wear red lipstick for the first time. Paul tells me I look like a million dollars.

When I walk out of the salon to meet Markus, he stares at me, and I smile.

"Wow!" he says.

I walk around to the passenger side. He recovers and rushes over to open my door. Once he is in the car, he touches my hair.

"It's not quite an afro, but this is how it looks naturally."

"It's beautiful."

"I know I won't be able to eat anything on the menu, but the way you look tonight, I want to take you somewhere special."

"I don't want to watch you starve. We did that last

Friday."

"Maybe I'll eat later if I'm lucky," he replies, winking at me.

He drives to a French restaurant, pulls up to the curb, and hands the keys to the waiting valet. We enter the restaurant, and everyone turns to look at us. My legs turn to jelly.

Markus takes my hand and talks to the Maître d'. I immediately regret having my hair like this, so I stare at the floor. The Maître d' offers us a table for two at the back of the restaurant.

My legs refuse to move. I try to emulate Markus as he is confident and poised. He does not let go of my hand as if he senses my distress.

We are finally seated, and I am relieved. I hold on to my tummy, willing the fluttery sensations away. My ears start to ring.

"Dylan, are you okay?"

"Why're they staring at us?"

Irrational tears prick my eyes, but the last thing I

want to do is cry here, where everyone can see. Our waiter arrives.

"Can we have a moment, please?" Markus tells her.

"Certainly, Sir."

She moves away, and he comes around the table. Squatting down to my level, he caresses my arms.

"They're staring at you because you're beautiful. I'm slowly realising that you have no idea how gorgeous you are."

He kisses me softly on my cheek before returning to his seat, and I try to relax.

I order the fish, and he orders soup with a salad. His salad arrives with anchovies, so he sends it back. I tell him that even I would reject that dish. The mushroom soup has heavy cream, so he eventually settles for the steamed vegetables. Yet again, he takes it all in his stride, and I am so impressed with his composure.

When we arrive back at my place, I make a fruit

and vegetable smoothie and offer him almonds. He sits at the dining table and devours the entire bag.

I sit across from him as he finishes his smoothie.

"This is the real reason you are so lean," I say, "Do you ever get angry?"

"Of course, I do," he says.

"When was the last time?"

"Today at work," he replies, and my eyes go wide.

"Why? What happened?"

He laughs at my expression.

"Someone didn't prepare for a meeting, even though it was scheduled a few weeks ago. I had to cancel my lunch date with you, and I wasn't happy about it."

I laugh, and he smiles. It is past midnight and way past my bedtime, but somehow, I am not tired. This change in my routine makes me nervous, but I don't dwell on it too much. I know what lurks beneath the murky surface of my mind, and I want to stay in my happy place.

Choosing Me

"I'm going to bed," I say.

He takes my hand, brings me around to his side of the table, and sits me on his lap. Slowly, he slides my zipper down. I stand and let the dress fall to the floor. My bleeding has stopped, but I want to shower before he touches me. I pick up my dress and kiss him.

"Will you stay?"

"Yes," he says, his eyes blazing.

I don't linger. While he is showering, I change the sheets and climb into bed. Making a mental note to buy sexy lingerie, as I am still sleeping in my cotton pyjamas. Impulsively, I decide to remove them and save him one job. The waiting triggers my arousal.

I know what is coming, and the anticipation is too much. I hear his electric toothbrush going, so I know he is almost finished.

I throw back the sheets and fondle my breasts. My nipples are painfully erect. He appears at the door and my hand stills. I bite my lower lip, slightly embarrassed.

"Don't stop. Try not to come," he says.

He sits on the bed, watching me as I touch myself. My hands move lower. I am looking at him, and he is focused on my hands.

He bends forward, sucking on my nipple, and I gasp. He does the same to the other one, alternating. My breathing is harsher. He moves slowly, moaning as he tugs gently. I take his hand and guide it lower.

"Dylan," he whispers, and I suddenly feel powerful.

He breathes heavily, and his fingers sink into my centre. I'm soaked.

"I want you now," I whisper.

He enters me slowly and stops. I realise that he does this so that I can adjust to the feel of him, and this thought makes me crazy with desire for this man. My hips gyrate, wanting to please him.

"Show me how you like it," I whisper.

"I like it like this. You feel good."

He closes his eyes and goes deeper, skin to skin.

"All of you, Markus. I want all of you."

I push up against him, and he cautiously goes in deeper, but I am impatient.

"Slowly, Dylan. I don't want to hurt you."

"I won't break. I want it harder."

My body curves, my legs opening wider, rubbing against him. My erect nipples graze his soft skin. I wrap my arms around his back, encouraging him. He slides inside more, and I hiss. His mouth falls onto mine, and he grinds faster. I am tipping over the edge; he and I, together.

He was holding back before, but now he gives me more. I love the feeling of everystroke. The muscles in his arms bulge, and he swears.

"Come inside of me. I want all of you."

I barely speak the words; I am drowning in a sea of carnal lust. I explode first, and the sensation lingers. My moan of sweet delight bounces off the walls. He follows, spilling into me, with my name on his lips as always.

He rolls over, pulling me on top of him. He holds me until my breathing returns to normal, and I fall asleep almost immediately.

* * *

My alarm goes off at five a.m. the next day. I groan as it goes to snooze. I swing my legs off the bed and groan again because I am sore between my thighs. I hurry to shower and dress. Halfway through making a breakfast smoothie, Markus finally shows up.

"Good morning," he says with a smile.

His usually groomed hair is dishevelled, and he does not seem to be in a hurry.

"Good morning," I reply chirpily.

My mood is soaring today. Toby's home for the weekend, and we are meeting for drinks later. My clock indicates that I have another half an hour before I must leave to catch my train. Yesterday, Markus dropped me off at my office and went to his apartment to shower and change. He apparently does not work for set hours; some Luck.

"That's an interesting outfit," he says.

I'm wearing black pants with suspenders and a cold-shoulder top with long sleeves.

He kisses my bare shoulder.

"Did you sleep well?" he asks.

I turn and kiss him quickly on his mouth.

"I did, but I must hurry now. I hate to be late."

I pour my smoothie into a glass and drink it down in one go.

"If you give me twenty minutes to shower and dress, I can take you to the office. I have the day off today."

I stop in my tracks.

Why did I not think of asking for the day off?

"Sure, but we need to leave before seven, as the traffic starts to build up," I say.

While he's in the shower, I change the sheets and catch up on some chores. We head out the door half an hour later.

"I won't be joining you for lunch today."

I try not to ask him what he's doing, although, I can't help but wonder if he's going to see *her*. I cave after only a few minutes.

"Doing anything nice on your day off?"

"I'm having some work done at the apartment, and then I'm meeting my mother for lunch. It's been in the diary for some time."

"That sounds nice," I say.

"I'd rather spend it with you," he says, and my heart skips a beat.

I smile to myself, remembering last night. He did not exaggerate; *sex feels much better every time.*

"Do you take any form of oral contraceptives?"

"No. We can use condoms."

"Yes, condoms do the job."

I decide to purchase some today since I don't have a lunch date. He is concentrating on the task at hand, so I pull out my phone and make notes in my calendar. A text comes in from Toby confirming the venue for our meet-up later.

"I'm meeting Toby after work. Will you be able to join us?" I ask, surprising myself.

"Yes, of course. If you'd like me to."

"I would."

He pulls up outside my office at ten to eight. He leans over, moving toward me very slowly and ever so softly, kisses me on my lips. Warmth spreads throughout my body.

"See you later," I say.

"Dylan, thank you for an amazing night."

My heart flips over, and I am not sure I will be able to walk straight, but somehow, I manage to step out of the car and walk around the front, crossing the road, but I feel his eyes on me.

At lunchtime, I scour the shops for condoms and lingerie. Spending an obscene amount of money on two gorgeous pieces in black and red, with matching heels.

My thoughts are about Markus all day.

This is not part of the plan.

My feelings confuse me. I am not sure if this is just fun anymore, but I don't know what to do about it.

I'm just not ready for it to end.

The time runs out, and I hurry back to the office. Markus sends me a text asking if he should pick me up. I text back to say I will meet them at the pub. I want to make up my time from lunch, and I also want to walk. Apart from our nightly activities, I've not exercised much this week.

I walk briskly toward the pub, buzzing with excitement to see Toby.

"Dylan!"

Toby shouts my name and rushes over to greet me at the door. He hugs me, spinning me in the air.

"You look fabulous. I love your hair like this!"

He fluffs my hair and gives me an odd look.

"You've had sex!"

The diners in the pub cheer and whistle.

Choosing Me

"Toby!"

I am mortified, but I laugh; I missed my buddy. We walk, arm in arm, back to the table where Markus is sitting and laughing.

"You went shopping without me?" Toby asks as he offers me a seat.

I sit next to him, and Markus looks at me. I want to kiss him, but I don't know how Toby will react.

"I went out at lunchtime today. I just bought a few bits."

I place my bags next to me on the seat.

"Toby, it's so good to see you," I take his hand, "When are you coming home?"

"I'll be back at the end of the month. I've been quite busy. This is top secret, but they want me to head up the team there, which is monumental. I'm struggling to find good people to do the work. I've recs that haven't been done for ages. It's a complete mess," he says.

"If you need some help, I can look at the figures

for you," I offer.

He looks at me consideringly.

"I could use your expertise, but I don't think Richard will be happy about it. He was always annoyed when you helped me in the past. You're the best he has; he'll have a headache if you go," he replies, taking a long swig of his beer.

"I can take some days off next week and help. Send me the files."

He kisses my cheek,

"You're too good to me. What are you drinking, the usual?" he asks.

Feeling tired from my busy week, I ask for something stronger.

"Can I have a cappuccino, please?"

He looks at me, raising his eyebrow.

"You want a coffee?"

"I was up quite late last night, and I'm tired."

"Okay, who is he?" Toby asks.

Choosing Me

My heart skips a beat.

"Who says it's a 'he'?" I reply.

"Fine, who is she?"

"Toby, I'll take this round," Markus says and stands.

He's wearing dark jeans with a crisp white shirt and looks incredibly sexy.

"Do you want the same?" Markus asks, and Toby gives him a thumbs up.

I link my fingers with Toby, and he touches my hair.

"I thought you hated this look."

He narrows his eyes at me, "I fancied a change."

"And seriously, you look good...different," he says, frowning slightly.

I try not to blush, but I know I have lost that battle.

"You look good too, Toby. I hope none of those handsome Germans have caught your eye. If you move away, I'm coming too."

I put my head on his shoulder.

He touches my hair with his free hand, "Don't worry. I'm not abandoning my girl."

Markus returns with our drinks. He puts my coffee next to me, and his fingers graze mine as he passes me a napkin. He passes Toby his drink.

He goes back to the bar again and returns with his drink.

"What are you having, Markus?" I ask.

I don't look at him when I ask this question as I am nervous that Toby will find out about us, and I haven't thought this far ahead.

"Watermelon fizz," he says.

Toby and Markus start chatting, and I listen intently to see if Markus will mention what he did today.

"What have you got in that bag?" Toby suddenly asks me, "Is that Victoria's Secret?"

"Dylan!"

"Toby, I was bored today at lunchtime, so I went

shopping. I needed a few things."

I try not to look at Markus but fail. When I do catch his eye, he smiles.

I give up and show Toby the contents of my bag.

"Nice."

To my relief, he doesn't pull the items out of the bag. I sip my coffee slowly.

"I have tickets to a party on the Thames tomorrow. I asked Dylan to accompany me, but you're more than welcome to join us."

I'd forgotten about that.

"Yes, sure, I'd like to. I have not stopped working since I landed in Munich," he gives me a sideways glance.

"D, you hungry?"

"Maybe something light."

"Markus, are you eating? I think they do have something for you, but I can check," says Toby.

"I'll take a look at the menu and then decide,"

Markus replies.

Toby releases me. He kisses me on my forehead and goes off to hunt for some food. It's the first time Markus and I have been alone since I arrived, and we lock eyes. I fight the urge to touch him, but he reaches his hands out and caresses my fingers.

Toby comes back with menus and olives for the table. I order chicken, and Toby orders a steak. Markus orders a mushroom burger without the sauce.

"Markus, the fries are okay to have. They're cooked in sunflower oil," I say.

He nods, smiling at me, and I head over to order his fries. It's my round, so I order more drinks for the table, switching to drinking water as the caffeine is making me buzz.

Taking the drinks to the table, I place Markus's glass in front of him.

"Thank you, Dylan," he gazes up at me.

I smile in return, and that is when I notice Toby looking at us. I take my seat; my heart is hammering.

Choosing Me

"Hey," I whisper.

I can see the wheels turning in his head, and I am so nervous that my bags fall to the floor.

"Should I put these in the car for you?"

"Yes, please," my voice shakes a little.

As soon as he leaves, Toby pounces on me, "Is there something going on with you two?"

Nervous, I sip my water, not meeting his eyes. He chuckles. Markus returns and sits across from us.

"Markus, are you two involved?" Toby's voice is incredulous.

I want to die right now.

Markus looks at me and exhales, "Yes."

"When did this happen?"

"Is it alright, Toby?" I ask.

"Of course, you don't need my permission. You can choose who you want to be with."

"I know, but he's your friend, so it makes it a bit different."

"Markus, are you sure you can handle this one?"

"She's a handful but worth it in the end."

The bell rings: our food is ready. I jump up and run over to pick it up before anyone else can. Looking over my shoulder, Toby and Markus are talking. I wonder what Toby is saying because Markus' face gives nothing away, as usual.

I take the meals over to the table, one at a time, checking the mushroom burger to make sure the chef did not add cheese or sauce.

"Bon Appetit!"

Toby cuts a piece of his steak and puts it on my plate.

"It's good," I say.

Markus offers me some of his fries. The mood at the table has shifted. Now that Toby knows about us, we are both more relaxed. It feels natural. We finish our meal, and Toby fancies something sweet. He leaves the table and brings over more drinks.

"Just popping to the loo," he says.

Choosing Me

I jump on the opportunity to sit next to Markus. He puts his hand on my thigh, and I kiss him. I had wanted to do that since I arrived. I move back to my seat just as Toby reappears. He eyes us up suspiciously. Markus and I start to laugh.

"What?" Toby asks, taking his seat.

I move over to be closer to him.

"It's like your third eye is on fire tonight," I reply, and he laughs.

Markus excuses himself and leaves the table.

"Toby, what should we do tomorrow?"

"Actually, I was thinking I'll fly back to Munich."

"No way, Toby. You said you were here for the weekend."

"I know, D, but I only came to see you, as I thought you'd be lonely. Obviously, you're not."

"I missed you, Toby. Please stay. I can just hang with you this weekend."

"No, D, it's good for you to be dating. I'm very pleased," Toby smiles widely and takes my hand.

"Really?"

"Yes. Markus will take care of you. Just don't break his heart. I happen to like him alot, and he's my only male friend," he says, laughing.

When Markus comes back, Toby tells him he will leave for Munich tomorrow.

"So soon? You should take a break. Stay for the weekend. Dylan missed you."

I flash Markus a huge smile to show my gratitude.

"Alright."

"How about some golf tomorrow?"

"Sounds good. You up for it, D?"

"No way. You two can go. I have loads of housework to catch up on," I regret it the moment I say it.

"Why is your housework not up to the usual standard?" Toby asks, grinning.

"No reason. I've been busy," I mumble.

The bell rings for his dessert.

Choosing Me

"Saved by the bell," he quips and goes to pick up his order.

I suggest we go for a walk along the riverside. We're quite close to the Strand, and I love walking along the embankment.

I walk between the two men, linking my arms with theirs. I am wearing my favourite comfortable wedged heel ankle boots, but Toby and Markus still tower over me. I suddenly stop walking, and they both look at me.

"What is it, D?"

"I'm happy," I say and walk on.

I can sense Toby rolling his eyes at Markus.

* * *

Shortly after midnight, Markus pulls up outside my apartment. He carries my bags and holds the door for me. I must have fallen asleep in the car as the last thing I remember is kissing Toby goodnight outside of the pub.

I feel a bit more revived after taking a hot shower.

Markus goes in after me. I really like this about him. I wrap my hair up on the top of my head and moisturise my body. I will have to sleep commando tonight. The new lingerie is for special occasions. When Markus comes into my room, he stops and stares at me.

"I'm behind on my washing. I've nothing to sleep in."

His trousers hang low on his hips. The effect is very sexy. He moves closer, running his hand down my back and over the curve of my bum.

"Your skin is like silk," he whispers against the hollow of my throat.

I close my eyes, savouring the feeling of his warm lips against my sensitive skin. He trails soft kisses down my back and up again. His touch is like molten heat, burning into my deepest core.

I turn my head so he can kiss me, and he does not disappoint. He consumes my every thought, and now, there is only him. I can no longer remember why I am in my closet.

Choosing Me

He drops to his knees in front of me, slowly unravelling my chords. He kisses my stomach and my thighs, sliding his hands over my calves. My breathing is erratic. His sweet kisses ignite my fire.

His hands wrap around my ankles, easing my legs wider. I lose my balance, but he grabs my hand.

"Hold on to me," he whispers.

I do hold on to him, as letting go would mean falling.

His tongue touches the softest part of me. If this is my sexual awakening, I am fully awake now, trembling with a hunger I never knew existed. I break, screaming loudly as my emotions take over.

I crumble; my legs can no longer keep me upright. He bears my weight, and I sob.

"Dylan!"

He tries to soothe me, lifting me in his arms and laying me on the bed. His lips are swollen, and I reach out to touch them. He grasps my fingers, kissing each one. I close my eyes while hot tears trail down my face.

"Markus," I whisper, still trying to recover, "That felt so good."

He smiles and presses his lips to mine.

"Can I do that to you?" I ask as he wipes away my tears.

"Will you show me how? I feel like I should return the favour to even things out," my voice croaks as I try to speak.

I roll slowly onto my side, facing him. He bends and kisses my breasts. His feather-light kisses are potent. My body floats as if he infuses sweet poison into my pores.

"Dylan, I'm here for you."

"I want it to be worth your time," I say breathlessly.

His fingers caress my hips and my stomach. His hands are everywhere, and I can barely speak.

"To have this with you is worth my time. It's beyond my wildest dreams. Trust me, Dylan, the pleasure of being with you is everything."

His voice is full of emotion, and I remember Toby's caution not to break his heart.

"I wondered today if you were going to see someone else."

"I had lunch with my mother. I told you that."

He looks away, and I sense he is not saying something.

"I know we're not exclusive, but will you tell me if you sleep with someone else?"

This is what worries me. He is so hard to read that I would never know if he were guilty. He nods but does not ask the same from me, but I say it anyway.

"I won't sleep with anyone else."

He closes his eyes and rolls onto his back, exhaling.

"You're not obligated to me. I can't make any demands," his eyes seem so sad when he speaks.

I only have one rule. No one is sad on my watch. Especially not if they're here in my bed. I straddle him, wobbling slightly. He sits up and steadies me. He is ready. His attention is on my full breasts, but I lift his face to see his eyes.

He helps me guide his erection slowly into my slickness. His hands shake a little, and I like it very much when he loses composure.

I follow his example and wait for my body to adjust to him. I push on him more as I want it all. My muscles feel stretched to the limit, but there is more of him. I, not being an expert on size, think he must come under the well-endowed category. I say this to him, and he laughs.

Euphoria bursts like bubbles inside my heart because his melancholy is gone, replaced by a feverish heat in his eyes. I rotate my hips in a circular motion, relishing the headiness of being in control. He reaches out to kiss me, but I don't want that.

"Just look at me, Markus," I whisper.

His perfect mask slips tonight, and, for the first time, I see the man behind it. He wants this. He says he is doing this for me, but I now know he needs this.

Choosing Me

With every thrust, I try to give him everything. This is all for him. He must notice the change as he tries to protest.

"Dylan, no," he whispers.

"Yes," I say to him, holding on and moving faster.

Despite my best intention, I start to waver. It's as if my energy is zapped away by my sole mission to please him, the way in which he does for me.

My thighs burn, and my thrusts grow weaker.

"Finish it, Markus," I beg him, "Take me the way you want to."

He hesitates for only a moment before he reacts. He rolls me onto my back and goes all the way in. As brief pain slices through me, my body arches and lifts off the bed, but I won't back down now. He goes wild, and his movements are frenzied.

His hand fondles my core as he slams into me, and my body bends to his will. My centre is oversensitive to his onslaught. He says my name and tells me that I'm beautiful.

We ride together to the highest point, and after, he crashes on top of me.

"Sorry," he says.

He is breathless and tries to roll away, but I hold him there. His breathing is erratic, and I listen to him as he tries to bring it under control. He rolls onto his back, falling asleep. I smile, giddy with my triumph. I kiss him and turn out the light.

Choosing Me

Mood Swings

The next day, Markus heads out to meet Toby for their game, and I start to clean my apartment, meticulously scrubbing until every surface gleams.

I tackle my spare bedroom last. It is the Master bedroom, but I sleep in the smaller room as it has a better view. Wheeling my sewing machine out of the closet, I dust it off carefully. It was Grams' most treasured possession, and it cost me a fortune to have it shipped to London.

The phone rings, and it's Kizzy. We chat for a while, and I put her on the speakerphone so I can work and talk.

"Are you out with Toby this weekend?"

I hesitate for the tiniest of seconds before responding. If Kizzy knew that I had finally experienced sex, she would give me her seal of approval. My sister has never had serious relationships, but my lips remain silent on that topic.

"We're going to a party tonight, and I've no clue what to wear."

"How about the dress you bought at Maxine's? I bet you haven't worn it yet."

"It's going to be cold."

"You can accessorise with fishnet tights and a short faux fur coat."

I dig in the closet for the outfit. It is still in its original packaging. The dress is black velvet with tiny spaghetti straps and a slit in the side that goes all the way up to my hip. It is the type of outfit that you can

Choosing Me

dress up or down.

After I hang up, I try on the dress, and it fits me perfectly. I may be the one to look like Grams, but my sister inherited her sense of style. She's a true fashionista.

When my sister walks into a room, she commands attention. She would have handled the restaurant situation on Thursday like a pro.

I leave the apartment to run errands. I buy fresh flowers from my local florist; this week, it's white Hydrangeas with green foliage. Then on to the supermarket, for a few items, before walking home. It is a balmy spring day. The skies are clear, and the sun is shining. Markus and Toby have picked a perfect day for golf.

After arranging the flowers, my apartment looks exactly as I like it. I make a salad with cold chicken for lunch. I want to eat now so I can still fit into my dress later.

I'm sitting at my sewing machine just after four p.m. when Markus arrives. He rings the buzzer, and I hurry over to let him into the building and open my front door, waiting until he comes up the stairs with the usual smile on his face. He is effortlessly gorgeous in faded blue jeans and a black t-shirt. He carries a clothes bag.

"Hey, beautiful," he says, leaning in for a kiss.

"Hey, did you have a good game?"

It's a moment before he answers, "Yes. I won!"

"Does Toby know you won?"

"Oh yeah, he knows."

"It looks very nice in here," he says, "What's this?"

"I was making some alterations. I usually buy my clothes too big and then adjust them, so they fit better."

He walks over and takes a closer look at my sewing machine. I'm bent over, sticking needles in my skirt, when he comes up behind me and touches my bum. I laugh and push him away, but he holds on to me.

Choosing Me

"Dylan, you're amazing. Is there anything you can't do?"

I don't have a chance to respond before he kisses me. I put my arms around his waist and stand on my tiptoes. He lifts me so I can reach up to his full height, and we both laugh.

"What's in the bag?" I ask.

"My suit for tonight," he replies, and I hang the bag in my closet.

"I went to my place to drop off my golf gear and shower."

"What time do we need to leave?"

"The boat sets sail at seven p.m. We need to arrive and park. Toby will meet us there. I would say we should leave by five thirty; give ourselves plenty of time."

I start packing up. I should begin getting ready, as we leave in an hour.

* * *

He is sitting in the lounge and looks up as I enter

the room.

"I'm ready," I say.

My dress is very flattering. I've added a glittery silver belt around my waist to match my sparkling silver Jimmy Choos. My hair falls in wiry spiral curls, framing my face. I've left it down as it will help to keep me warm.

He walks slowly around me, taking in my outfit from every angle.

"You are perfection," he whispers and kisses me.

He looks pretty good too. His outfit is all black, with a dress shirt, pants, and a slim black tie. I grab my coat and clutch, and we head out for our night in the town. Markus holds my hand and helps me down the stairs as my heels are ridiculously high. He opens the car door, and I slide in elegantly. He notices the slit in my dress when he sits on the driver's side.

He smiles, shakes his head, and starts the engine. I laugh as he reverses out of the drive and joins the traffic heading into London.

Choosing Me

Toby meets us at the entrance to the boat. He is gorgeous in his all-white ensemble. His mouth falls open when he sees me. Markus and I hold hands, walking toward him. At first, I was a little reluctant when he reached out to take my hand, but it feels right tonight.

"D, you look sensational," Toby gasps and gives me a kiss.

"Why have I never seen this dress before?" says Toby as I link my arms with both men.

"I bought it in Boston and completely forgot about it."

"It was made for you," he says.

"Thanks, Toby."

They both indicate for me to go first, so I carefully step onto the boat as it wobbles slightly.

Once we set sail, I wonder how I've never done this before. The experience of sailing past the London sites and seeing the city from the river at night is a rite of passage.

We are standing on the deck, and I'm wearing my coat, but it's still windy and cold. I'm warm enough, though. Toby and Markus shield me from the wind. I have one arm draped around Toby, and Markus holds my other hand. I want to remember this moment forever.

When the boat reaches the end and starts making its way back up the river, we head inside to enjoy the music and warm up. There is hot food being served, but I'm not hungry.

Markus goes off to mingle; he knows people on board, so Toby and I spend most of the night together.

Throughout the evening, I sense that Markus is looking at me, and whenever I'm brave enough to chance a glance at him, his eyes meet mine, and he smiles brilliantly. My cheeks heat up, and I avert my eyes.

"D, what have you done to my friend?"

Toby sits next to me, nibbling on finger foods.

"He's head over heels in love with you."

Choosing Me

Toby chews, not looking at me, and I smack him playfully.

"No, he's not. We're just having fun together."

"*You* are having fun. He is serious. Trust me."

"He's not exactly free; he loves another woman," I reply softly, trying not to reveal how I truly feel about this.

I don't know how much Toby knows, but he shrugs.

"I love you, but I don't want to have a sexual relationship with you. There are lots of ways you can love someone."

I cling to Toby's words, wanting them to be true.

"Just keep doing whatever you're doing because it's working," he leans in and kisses my cheek.

I change the subject.

"Are you going to stop eating? I want to dance."

"You're here with two men," he replies, putting more food in his mouth.

"Toby, stop making trouble," I scowl at him.

Usually, I don't wait, I'm happy to hit the dance floor by myself, but this is not really that type of party.

"Markus can dance, go ask him."

"He can?"

"Yes, his mom is a professional dancer, so he had dance lessons and everything. The lads used to tease him about it. How is it you don't know that? What do the two of you talk about?"

I turn, giving him a look.

"Oh, Come on. TMI, D," he holds up his hand, laughing.

"You asked."

Toby eventually gives in, as I knew he would, and we make our way to the dance floor, throwing shades to the funky tunes. As usual, he attracts the eye of the female guests, who don't seem to care that he already has a dance partner. He laughs and obliges, so I mostly dance on my own.

That is until a familiar set of arms encircle my

waist and spin me around. "Can I have this dance?"

The band plays an upbeat song, but he holds on to me, and we rock slowly. I can sense he is looking at me, but I don't dare meet his eyes. Another song comes on, and he starts to groove. His hips sway to the tempo of the song.

Dancing along with him is so much fun. Watching him come alive. He really can move, but I guess I should have known by the way he moves in bed. I blush now, just thinking about it.

My heated cheeks intensify with every glance. It doesn't help that he is looking at me as if he knows exactly what I'm thinking.

The boat docks at midnight, and there is a firework display. A perfect grand finale to an amazing evening.

Someone had taken a photograph of us three earlier. In the picture, Toby is standing beside me, I have my arm around his waist, and he has his arm around me. Markus is holding my other hand. Toby is pointing ahead, saying something, and I'm smiling, but Markus is looking at me. I am so grateful to have this photograph, as this is one of the happiest nights of my life.

Toby is drunk and singing at the top of his voice, so we decide it's time to take him home. It's an interesting car journey. I sit in the back with Toby, holding a sick bag at the ready, as Markus is nervous Toby might throw up in the car.

We make it to Toby's place without any mishaps, and he helps Toby into his apartment.

"He's going to have a nasty headache in the morning."

"I've never seen him like that. He must really be stressed. I think at one point I saw him snogging a woman; Toby never behaves like this."

I am a bit concerned, but Markus just laughs, and it is such a beautiful sound that I join in. We arrive home at two a.m. As soon as we enter my apartment, Markus pounces and starts kissing me.

"Dylan, I want you while you're still wearing that dress," he whispers.

Choosing Me

He must see the panic on my face as I never touch my bed unless I'm washed. He removes my heels, takes my hand, and leads me to the lounge.

He sits on the couch, gazing up at me with his irresistible eyes. He starts slowly undressing me. He removes my tights. He runs his hands up and down my bare legs, his eyes travelling up my body. He kisses my core through my panties, and I'm nervous. I've been dancing all night, so I must be sweaty. I don't think I'll enjoy this. I try to pull away, and he pulls me back.

He sits back on the couch and pulls me on top of him. I'm still wearing my dress. His fingers push my panties to the side, and he penetrates. He does not give me the usual time to adjust. The moment he is inside me, he moves with fierce, powerful strokes. The tempo is fast, and I am always one step behind, playing catch-up.

He palms my face and kisses me with urgency as if he senses this, and I am fired up. It's like a switch goes off in my brain, and suddenly I'm wild with wanting him. I pull down the top of my dress to free my breasts and cry out when his teeth graze against my hardened nipples. I lean backwards to prolong the sensations, but he hits the spot inside me, and I detonate.

A scream rips through my throat as the cool liquid fills my insides, so I know he, too, is at the end.

He holds on to me, and we stay like this for what seems like forever, panting feverishly. My heart is beating too fast, and the feeling is a little scary until I notice the pulse on his neck beating in time with my heart.

I find the energy to move off him; my legs are stiff. He goes off to clean himself and comes back to clean me. He adjusts my dress and pulls me onto his lap.

"Why did you scream? Did I hurt you?"

"No, it felt so intense," my voice is hoarse,

"You were incredible. Every time is better than the last."

"Dylan, being with you erases everything I thought I knew. I've never had sex like this before."

Choosing Me

"Really?"

"Yes, really," he says.

He opens his eyes, and I press my lips to his. He deepens the kiss, and I feel his arousal. I smile and stand up. Pulling my dress over my head, I drop my panties and strapless bra to the floor.

I unbutton his shirt and run my hand over his chest. His breathing changes, and he helps me by removing his shirt and dropping it to the floor. I unbutton his trousers, he stands, and I watch as they fall.

Impulsively, I lie on the rug on the floor and open my legs as far apart as they will go. His eyes go wide, I assume with shock, and it would have been comical if the need was not so immediate.

He falls to his knees and enters me swiftly; I cry out for more. It's like I'm a woman possessed, and only he can cure me. I am loud, and my neighbours might be getting an earful, but I can't stop myself, and he does not seem to want to stop either.

He knows when I'm nearly there and kisses me,

so my scream lodges in my throat. He finishes in a more dignified manner, and it's the last thing I remember before I lose consciousness.

I wake the next day, sprawled across his chest. He must have put the blanket over me in the night. I open my eyes and look around at the scene. I'm so embarrassed that I don't attempt to meet his eyes.

I stand up, pick up the clothes, put them away in the spare room, and go straight to the shower. It is already past ten thirty, and I'm famished. I spend a long time under the hot water.

I wash my hair and brush my teeth twice to make up for last night. I go to my bedroom and close the door.

I hear Markus turn on the shower a few minutes later. I dress in light blue distressed jeans, an oversized white blouse, and a black and white checked waistcoat. I use gel and water to slick my hair back into a wavy bun.

I finally feel ready to brave the kitchen to hunt for food. I make a protein smoothie. Markus comes in as

Choosing Me

I pour the smoothie into two glasses. He helps himself to a banana from the fruit bowl. I know he is looking at me, but I'm not relenting. I take a bowl of roasted almonds from my cupboard to put out on the table. Markus blocks my path and tilts my chin up, so I have no choice but to meet his eyes.

"So, you lost control and had a night of wild sex. This is not a crime," his fingers caress my lips,

"You wanted to experience sex, and this is all a part of it."

"Do you think the neighbours heard me?"

"I think the entire neighbourhood heard you."

He takes the nuts and puts them on the table. I sit and finish my smoothie, and he's still smiling.

"Markus, this is super embarrassing."

I bite my thumb nail. He removes my hand from my mouth.

"You were super sexy, and no one got hurt. I had to save you from banging your head against the coffee table at one point, but apart from that, harmless fun."

***

Toby and I meet up at the market. He looks a little worse for wear.

"D, tell me what I did last night. No, don't tell me. I woke up this morning, and my mouth tasted like dirty old socks."

I laugh and decide to put him out of his misery.

"It was probably the Johnny Walker. You had a fair bit."

"That would explain this massive headache. Why did you let me drink like that?"

He stops suddenly, and I walk into him.

"Markus said it was a good idea for you to let your hair down."

"D, I have no hair, I'm a bald man, purely by choice, of course, but when I'm out with you, I expect you to look out for me," he says, putting a jar of organic honey in my basket.

"I apologise. It won't happen again."

I reach up to kiss him on the cheek, and he smiles.

Choosing Me

"How about I make you a sweet potato pie to make up for my lapse?"

I use Grams' recipe, and this is his absolute favourite.

"All will be forgiven, D."

I go hunting for the ingredients.

"What is Markus up to today?"

We are walking arm in arm along the regents' canal, heading back to his place with our spoils from the market. This is becoming a sore point for me, but I pretend to be blasé about it.

"He said he was going to visit his sister."

"What, don't you believe him?"

"It doesn't matter anyway. He's free to do whatever he wants."

Toby stops walking, but this time I anticipate it.

"D, I wish you wouldn't. You care for him. Why do you pretend otherwise?"

I start walking again, and he lets me go. One of the

things I like about Toby is that he never presses an issue. He'll wait patiently until I am ready to talk about it. Safe in that knowledge, I change the subject.

"What time do you leave tomorrow?"

"I'm flying out first thing."

We take the tube back to his place in Greenwich.

I love Toby's place. It's small but completely open plan. When I first moved to London, I wanted a place just like this. For me, this is one dream I hope to achieve. I'd love to have my own place in the city.

I think about Markus' apartment in Canary Wharf. I'd never admit it to anyone, but it is quite spectacular. It seems rather unfair that Toby was better than Markus at school, but Markus could afford a nicer place.

If Toby lived in America, he would be making triple of what he makes now. He could make out like a bandit. He would be the one driving a fancy car and living in a penthouse in the sky.

I look at my beautiful friend, and I wish him all

that. He comes from humble beginnings. Toby never knew his father, and his mother, Gina, raised him on her own. She moved back to Jamaica only last month. Toby bought her a house over there. We have plans to visit her together one day.

I go to the kitchen and start prepping for the pie. Toby is working on his laptop at his dining table. I prepare a large garden salad once the pie is in the oven. We spend the next hour going over the files, and I'm confident I can help him. I stop to take the pie out of the oven. The kitchen smells heavenly. I tell him to password-protect and save the files on the shared drive, and I'll work on them for him next week.

"D, you're too good to me."

"Hungry?"

"Starving. That smells amazing."

Toby eats his pie and salad, washing it down with water. I laugh as he usually has a glass of wine with his dinner, but I guess his head is still sore from last night's excursions. I remember my own evening and blush.

"I'll pack the rest of the pie so you can take it for lunch tomorrow if you like."

He wants to have an early night as he will have to be up at four a.m. to catch his flight, so I text Markus to tell him I'm ready. The slow dread of melancholy descends.

"When will you come again, Toby?"

"I'm not sure."

"I know this is a good opportunity for you, but I'll be sad if it changes things between us," I say.

"D, I'm always here for you. I'll come if you need me, or you can come to me. Besides, you've got Markus now, so you won't be lonely. I'll be back before you know it," he links his fingers with mine.

"Can you just do one thing? Give Markus a chance. Try not to shut him out. Trust me; he's one of the good ones."

His face is serious, so I nod my head.

I want to ask him why he thinks Markus is so

Choosing Me

good, but the buzzer to his building rings.

Toby lets Markus in, and I observe the two of them together. Markus always seems so relaxed around Toby, laughing and joking. I busy myself in the kitchen, and he comes over to say hello. He kisses me openly in front of Toby. If he senses my mood, he doesn't let it show.

I suddenly realise that this annoys me. He always seems so calm and controlled. I can never tell what he is thinking. He is guarded and secretive.

I wonder how these two are friends. They seem to have so little in common and are from completely different social backgrounds.

Markus seems to effortlessly glide through his life, while Toby works twice as hard just to progress his career. I'm upset about not being able to see him every day at work.

By the time we head back to my place in Markus' car, my mood has turned from blue to black. I don't say much, and he doesn't ask. He turns on the radio. The music helps, and I sing along to my favourite songs.

When we arrive at my place, I open my apartment door and leave it open. I hear it when he closes it softly. I take my shopping from the market to the kitchen and start unpacking, then head to the shower and go through my routine, changing into tights and an oversized comfortable hoodie that reads 'Syracuse'.

I go to the spare room to organise clothes for the week ahead. Keeping busy helps to distract me, so when that's done, I put my new lingerie on a gentle hand wash cycle, then make a salad for tomorrow's lunch. Once the cycle finishes, I hang the lingerie on the airer in my lounge.

I'm out of ideas. I go back to my spare room and start cleaning, even though I'd cleaned it yesterday.

I could do my alterations, but I try not to do that when I'm upset. It involves lots of needles, and I don't want to leave one lying around. That could be fatal.

He stands at the door, silently observing me, but I don't want to speak first. I've no idea what he's been doing, but he has changed into sweats as well. His hair appears to be damp, so he must have been in the shower. I go into the walk-in closet and start refolding already-folded clothes.

I need therapy.

"Hi," he says, walking into the room.

"Can I talk to you for a minute?" he asks politely.

I glance over at him, and my heart accelerates as panic sets in.

This is it; he's leaving. He's fed up with my childish behaviour.

Toby's words come back to me.

"Yes, of course."

I switch off the light in the closet and sit on the bed. He sits next to me and puts an envelope on my lap. I don't touch it.

"Open it," he coaxes, "It's for you."

I open the envelope. Inside is an open plane ticket in the name of Miss Dylan Francine Weekes from London Heathrow to Munich International. It's a first-class ticket.

"When did you do this?"

"I bought it today and printed it back at my place."

I don't know what to say.

"I know you miss him."

"Thank you, this is really sweet."

"I'm sorry about my mood earlier," I say, eating my humble pie, "I do miss Toby."

I can't look Markus in the eye as shame consumes me. He bends over, picks up something, and passes it to me. It's four hardback novels tied with a yellow ribbon.

"What's this?" I ask, smiling.

"Tolkien, Lord of the Rings series. My sister had these at her house. They were mine from junior school. I thought we could read them together."

He unties the ribbon and takes out the hobbit. I put the plane ticket on the dresser and scoot over to the corner of the bed. He sits next to me and pulls me closer. He opens the book and starts to read.

Choosing Me

With my head on his chest and his beautiful voice bringing the story to life, I fall asleep.

Only while sitting at my desk the next day do I realise we didn't have sex, and I enjoyed being with him.

When I woke up this morning, the day was bright and sunny. Markus drove me to work. I was wearing my green suede pumps. I smile, remembering how he could not take his eyes off my legs during the car journey.

Now, it's pouring rain. We'd planned to meet in the park for lunch, and I have the salad I prepared last night all boxed up. I sigh and look at the sheets of rain.

Well, it is April. I guess I'll just go to the canteen.

I'm working on Toby's files, so I don't notice the time. My phone rings, making me jump. Markus' name flashes on the screen.

"Hi."

I figure he is cancelling the lunch date as the rain is pouring.

"Hello, Dylan. I'm outside. Are we still on for lunch?"

I look out the window, and the rain is coming down in sheets.

"I'll be down in a minute."

I change into boots as I have pairs of shoes in my desk drawer for scenarios like this, and I can't afford to ruin my suede shoes. I don't have a raincoat, but I suspect Markus might have his car.

I hurry downstairs, and he is there, waiting for me. When he sees me, he comes out of the car with a large umbrella. I run out to meet him. He pulls me under the umbrella and helps me into the car.

He drives to a small café, parking up across the road. He holds the umbrella over us and puts his arm around me as we cross the quiet street.

I am nostalgic the moment I enter the café. They're serving clam chowder and playing music from a popular sitcom I used to watch as a child.

"What is this place?"

Choosing Me

"It's a New England café, and I thought you'd like it."

He picks out a booth-style table, and we sit down. There is a steady lunch crowd. I smile at the couple next to us.

"It reminds me of home, but what will you have?"

I think of the packed lunch back at work.

"I had a very substantial breakfast, so maybe that will keep until dinner?"

I scour the menu to see what is suitable for him, but the ingredients are all wrong.

"Markus, why would you come to eat at a place where there is nothing on the menu you can eat? That's just nuts."

"I thought it would cheer you up," he says as the waitress comes over to take our order.

She is all perky, "Hi there, what can I get you today?"

I ask about the options for Markus, and they have nothing, so I tell her we are not staying after all.

"Come on. Let's go," I say.

He apologises to the waitress, and we head back out into the rain.

"This feels like an adventure," he says.

"I have a perfectly suitable packed lunch back at work. I'm allowed to have a visitor, so we can eat in the restaurant."

* * *

Much later, back at home, I cook tofu for the first time, and I'm baffled. Markus is no use, so I improvise, and the result is nasty, so I make myself fried chicken.

He tells me he enjoys his dinner, but I have my doubts. I cut into my warm chicken and make pleasurable sounds as I chew.

"Markus, I don't know how you go through every day, never being sated."

"I make up for it through other avenues," he replies.

"You know you don't have to babysit me every

day. You're free to go off to do whatever you were doing before."

He stares intensely as if he is trying to imprint my face into his memory, "Have you had your fill of me?"

"I've had my introduction to sex, and you were a very good teacher. Hopefully, I was an excellent student."

I joke with him simply to stir up a reaction.

"There's still room for improvement. Practice makes perfect," he winks at me, "Which reminds me, when will I see you in your new lingerie?"

"I tell you what, you wash up for me, and it just might be your lucky night."

He goes to do his duty, and I switch on the laptop I borrowed from work. I've been working two jobs today, trying to help Toby with his extra workload.

Markus seems preoccupied when he comes over and sits at the table next to me. I carry on working as I want to send this off tonight. When I glance at him, he is looking at me. I smile and reach out my hand,

and he links our fingers.

"You, ok?" I mouth to him, and he smiles.

I email Toby to let him know the documents are saved in the shared drive and switch off the laptop.

I sense that Markus wants to talk, so I give him my full attention, "Sorry. What's up?"

"I worry about you. You seem different from the girl I first met. I wondered if it's me, this, us, that causes your capricious behaviour."

"I'm moody by nature. I've always been this way. I sometimes wonder if this is the right thing to do with you. I like being with you. I feel safe with you."

"It's nice to know that. At times it seems almost like you resent me."

"I don't resent you. I just can't help feeling like your world and mine are very different."

"Is that a bad thing?"

"You're Caviar, and I'm ice cream."

"Which flavour of ice cream?"

Choosing Me

"I don't know, Chocolate."

"Dairy-free, I hope."

"Yes. Of course."

I smile, but he is quiet for a while, rubbing his thumb across the back of my hand.

"I don't care much for Caviar, but I love chocolate ice cream."

I stare at him, shaking my head.

"I was speaking metaphorically," I say, and he smiles,

"I don't think we're so different."

"Trust me, we are. It's no wonder I'm so nervous around you. Your demeanour screams upper crust. You've got this whole 'Finest range' thing going on. You ooze confidence no matter where you are; the man who has it all."

His eyes bore into mine.

"I don't have everything, Dylan. I would trade all that I own to make you mine."

Revelations

I don't expect this, so I just stare at him, speechless. His eyes are like melting orbs. "Markus, I didn't realise you felt this way,"

I stumble through the words, my voice trembling.

"I don't say that to scare you or make you feel obligated to reciprocate. I know how to live my life wanting."

His words surprise me. I imagine him to be the type of man for whom doors simply open.

"I shouldn't be complaining," he says, touching my fingers.

"Are you saying you're unhappy with your life?"

"We started talking about you."

"My mood swings are a part of who I am. They go just as fast as they come, but they don't define me. At the end of the day, I'm very happy with my life."

"I know you're happy. It's the reason I worry. It would kill me if I somehow messed that up, pulled you into my..."

"Complications?"

"Exactly. You're so wholesome and good. I've stumbled upon a real treasure, more valuable than all the money in the world. I'm regretful for the things in my past that I wish I could erase; decisions I'm not so proud of."

"Like what?"

His eyes look conflicted. This feels like a moment of truth. I always sense there are things he does not say to me but wants to. I shy away from hearing them.

I don't want to admit that my mood swings have worsened since I met him. They usually come on when I'm afraid or feeling like I'm not in control of my emotions. It's how I keep myself grounded. I shut everything out and become paranoid, emotional, and neurotic. The pain becomes my sanctuary. I trust it because I know it well.

I take a deep breath and try to be brave, "Is this about her?"

He shakes his head, "No. This is about you."

My heart is hammering in my chest. I want to ask what about me, but I'm afraid of what he'll say.

"I know I'm temperamental, but it's really my defence mechanism."

I don't want him to regret our time together.

"Honestly, Markus, when you peel back the layers, underneath it all, I'm just a girl looking for the same thing as every other girl out there."

He stares at me for the longest time.

"I wanted you from the moment I first saw you. I

would have settled for just being in your company, but you kissed me, and since then, I've been struggling with right and wrong."

Once again, he removes his mask. This is not like the last time when it merely slipped off. Tonight, he does it deliberately. I can't look away from his face.

"You once spoke to me about choices. The idea was evocative to me. I knew that I would want more than just one car journey with you, but Dylan, the reality is that you're free, and I'm not. The more time I spend with you only exacerbates the situation. I know what I should do, but it's conflicted with what I want to do."

His melancholy hangs like a dark cloud.

"What do you want to do?"

"Keep you."

I immediately go to him, sit on his lap, and put my arms around him. I want him to show me his beautiful smile.

"You can have me for as long as you want."

"No.... don't say that. You've already given me so much of yourself."

"Do you mean my virginity?"

"Yes. I should have insisted that you save yourself for a man who deserves you. A man who could tell you he loved you when making love to you for the first time."

"It was a most beautiful experience, and yes, maybe we weren't in love, but I certainly felt loved," I say.

He kisses me. Slowly, softly, with his hands on the nape of my neck. Our lips interlock, and it's as if I am melting, his warmth heating my blood, his heart beating in time with my own.

This kiss feels more intimate. I imagine this is how he would kiss me if I could tell him I love him.

"Don't move," I whisper, breaking the kiss.

It is time to lighten the mood. I remove my flowers from the table, replace them with four lit large candles, and switch off the lights.

Choosing Me

"I'll be right back," I say.

He looks mysterious, sitting in the soft candlelight. I've already showered, so I slip on my new black lingerie.

I stare at myself in the full-length mirror.

This thing looks scandalous.

It fits me like a glove, pulling everything in. The material is sheer, so I can see my body through it. I never knew I could look this sexy.

The satin heels complete the look. My legs appear long and shapely. Feeling nervous, I exhale and go back to join him.

He looks up when I enter the room and closes his eyes briefly, exhaling sharply.

"Oh my, Dylan."

His voice drifts over to me, and my nerves disappear. The light from the candles sets the mood perfectly. I put on some music, and George Michael's "Jesus to a Child" comes on my stereo. I turn to face him.

"Would you like to dance?"

He walks over to me and takes my hand. I meet his gaze without a flicker. Standing taller, no longer feeling shy or unsure.

I suppose when a man tells a woman he would love to make her his, she feels powerful. He holds me, and we rock slowly to the music. I look at us in my wall mirror, the lit candles adding drama to the moment. Our skin glows, and we are beautiful together.

What I especially love about this moment with him is that, even though I'm dressed provocatively, he dances while gazing into my eyes.

He doesn't touch me in a sexual way. When the song ends, I kiss him, and as our tongues touch, he moans softly.

I break the kiss, pulling out one of my dining chairs and sitting him on it. His eyes, darkened with desire, roam over my body, beautifully enhanced by my lingerie. His hands explore every inch of me, gliding down my legs, over my torso and breasts.

Choosing Me

He pulls me closer, breathing me in. Our reflection in the mirror heightens my senses, making me feel sexy beyond belief. When I unhook the clasps covering my modesty, he does not hesitate.

With his mouth hot and full, he kisses deep into my core. The candles, the heels, and the view of him devouring me in the mirror; I climax almost immediately. Whimpering, I fall onto his lap.

He lifts me with ease and takes me to my room. He undresses in record time and tells me we need to use condoms for a while now, before pausing to slip one on. He enters me, and we both cry out at the same time.

He wants to keep me...

With wild abandon, I give myself to him. I want to drive him crazy; I want him to only want me, and I want to *erase* her memory or any other woman he has ever had.

He rips my lingerie in an urgent need to get to my breasts. I help him pull it down, and he tugs gently with his lips. My body is on fire, and only he can quench my desire.

I want to tell him that I'm his to keep forever, but his kisses drown out the sound, so I show him instead, laying myself bare and surrendering to him as we collide.

* * *

"Sorry about your lingerie. I'll replace it," his voice brings me back to reality.

He climbs back on the bed and pulls me into his arms, spooning me.

"I think that's what's supposed to happen. It must be how they make money," I'm exhausted, and my voice is croaky.

"I'd like to visit the Shire now, please, to check on my favourite hobbit."

"He's your favourite?" he asks.

He smooths my hair back and kisses my eyes, nose, and lips.

"Mm," I respond, as his touch is everything.

He runs his hands down my body.

"Sure, but I'm not quite finished with you yet," he says with his hands between my thighs.

"Do you mind if I turn you over?" he whispers.

He opens another packet, lifts me by my stomach, and pushes my bottom onto his legs.

He runs his hands down my back, and I sink my head into my pillow, feeling deliciously exposed as he enters me slowly. He exhales, and I hold my breath.

"Try to relax, Dylan."

I release my held breath, but as he sinks deeper, my body tenses as the pain shoots right through me. Gritting my teeth, I persevere, but he stops.

"Am I hurting you?"

"Yes," I say as he pulls out, turning me over and hugging me.

"Sorry."

"I know it's the position you like, but I can't. It just hurts."

"What does the pain feel like?"

"It feels like you're too deep and hitting something inside me."

I hold on to my tummy and the residual pain. He inspects it, and I groan. It's not the best part of me. He kisses the spot where I had the pain, and I giggle before quickly rolling away.

"Stop, seriously. I don't want you lingering there."

"Why not?" he asks.

Yeah, we're not having that conversation.

"You should see a gynaecologist about this, Dylan. It may be something they can fix."

"Heaven forbids I'm unable to do doggy style."

"I'm only thinking of you," he shakes his head, "Besides, it's not my favourite position."

He pulls me closer and kisses my hair, smoothing it back in his signature move.

"What is then?"

"When I can kiss you and see you reacting to my touch," his fingers caressing lightly.

"What's yours?"

"I like it when you kiss my, um..." I say, suddenly going speechless from shyness.

"Yes, that is rather enjoyable," he runs his fingers along my inner thigh, and I shudder.

"Did she teach you that as well?" I ask him softly.

He doesn't answer at first.

"I've only done that with you."

"You've been together for so long, and you've never done that with her?"

"We did other things," he admits, and I sense he doesn't want to talk about it, but I persist.

"Did you enjoy sex with her?" I ask softly.

"Yes, I did. She was very good."

My heart sinks, but I smile, "That's nice."

"It feels different with you, Dylan."

I want to tell him this line is not very original, but instead, I ask, "Different, how?"

He hesitates, and I think he doesn't want to say.

"I feel you here," he says, indicating his heart.

I have no words.

He kisses me on the forehead.

Later, I clean up in the bathroom, changing into my cotton pyjamas. I fetch the novel from my spare room while he is in the shower.

He opens the book to our page, and I snuggle up next to him as he transports me to a magical place for the second time tonight.

***

"You know, Dylan, this commute would be twenty minutes tops from my place, and that's during rush hour."

"What's your point?"

"I love those looks of yours," he says, pulling up to my building. It took longer than usual to arrive today.

"Thank you for the lift." I prepare to leave, but he pulls me toward him for a kiss, "Have a great day, beautiful. I'll see you tonight."

Choosing Me

Waiting to cross the street, I glance over my shoulder, smiling to see him checking me out. Blowing him a kiss, I run across to the entrance. Due to work commitments, I won't see him for lunch, but I'll accompany him to a football game tonight.

We haven't spoken about our relationship's progress since his big reveal on Monday, but I'm feeling anxious. I want to talk to Toby, but he is busy with work, and the quicker he can finish, the faster he can come home.

As I sit in the park and enjoy the sunshine, my cell phone rings. My salad bowl is empty as my nightly activities have increased my appetite. I check the caller ID and smile.

"Hey, Toby, I was just thinking about you."

"Hey, D, I wanted to thank you for all your help. You did great work," he sounds like he's right next to me, and it's so good to hear his voice.

"You're welcome. When are you coming home?"

"Well, D, they've offered me the role of global CFO."

"What? Are you serious?" I scream, and a few people look over at me.

This is such good news.

"I know, D, it's... I'm speechless."

I can hear the relief in his voice.

"You're my boss! I'm so proud of you."

"I can't wait to tell Markus. He's going to be thrilled for you."

"Things going okay with you two?"

"Toby, this is your moment. We will celebrate when you come home."

"Yes, we will. I'll call you soon, okay? Hey D, call me if you need to talk or whatever."

We say goodbye and hang up.

Later, I share the news with Markus, and he seems so genuinely pleased for Toby, it touches me, so I hold his hand as we walk into the Football stadium. I flirt with him and kiss him in public. It's just such a happy day, and I'm feeling giddy.

Choosing Me

Football is a mystery to me, but I think his team has won, as he's in good spirits. He takes me to the players' box to meet one of the players. I've no idea who is who, but he explains that Alan Robinson is the biggest football player in the UK.

"He can't be that big if I've never heard of him."

"He's legendary."

"Is he cute?"

Markus points to a huge billboard, "That's him."

Oh, my!

"Yep, he's cute."

"Would you like to meet him?" he asks, grinning.

"Why would I want to meet him?"

"To say congratulations and also to thank him for the tickets."

"You know him?"

"Alan's my client. I help him with his branding. He gave me the tickets," he says, reaching for my hand.

"Sounds like bribery to me," I say.

We arrive at the box, and a few people are already there. I don't like this much, so I let go of Markus' hand and stand away from the crowd.

"You go. I'll wait here," I say, but he does not budge.

"Markus!" I hear someone call out.

He goes off to greet his client, and I look out the glass to the stadium below. It's impressive from this vantage point.

"Who's that?" says a voice.

I crane my neck, trying to see above the heads of the crowds, but they soon part, and I notice the footballer. Alan approaches me and offers his hand.

"Hi," he says.

"Hey," I reply.

"We haven't been introduced. I'm Alan, and you are?"

His eyes are on my breasts.

Choosing Me

Ugh, I hate this.

"I'm here with my boyfriend."

"Alan, I hope you're not harassing my woman," says Markus as he approaches, "I charge extra for that."

"Markus, this is your lady? I apologise. You should keep a tighter rein on her. Someone could run off with her," he smiles, offers me his hand again, and I shake it.

"Nice to meet you," I say.

"The pleasure is all mine."

We leave shortly after.

"I hope I haven't lost you your client."

"I don't think so, besides, I especially liked the part when you said I was your boyfriend."

"It's what I say when I'm out with Toby, so any guys hitting on me would back off."

"That's major," he says, laughing.

"I'm not following you. It's far too late for me to

understand your riddles."

"Taking Toby's place as your protector. I've been upgraded."

I laugh. I wouldn't admit it, but I do like the idea of him being my protector. But I'm not letting down my guard; my walls are up, and they're not coming down.

* * *

I don't sleep very well for the next few days. I'm not sure why, but I keep waking at random hours. This is especially awful for me as it makes me cranky, and I tend to snap at Markus as he is with me most of the time.

He says I wake him up when I'm restless, but I don't notice this. I always think he sleeps like the dead. Last night, I managed only four hours of sleep, and today, I'm snarling like an angry beast.

I become particularly aggressive when he asks me a question. He never loses his patience with me, so when he slams the lid of his laptop, it reverberates, and I know he's had enough.

Choosing Me

"Dylan, what's wrong?"

"Nothing," I say in my chirpiest voice, "I didn't sleep very well."

He gazes at me and sighs, walking over to sit beside me on the couch. The weather is nice and mild today. My windows are thrown wide, and the sunlight is streaming into my lounge.

My neighbourhood is leafy and green. Markus and I went to the park earlier as I wanted him to show me some running skills. We've been inseparable since the day he told me he wanted to keep me.

"You know you can talk to me about anything, right?"

"I know."

This irrational fear and guilt chip away at my walls. I don't want to admit, even to myself, that I never want to let him go. I inch closer to kiss him, but he stops me.

"Is this too much?"

"No," I answer too quickly.

"Are you sure?"

"It's probably just that time of the month."

"PMS?"

I nod and laugh, but he does not laugh with me. He runs his hand down my ponytail.

"I'm going to Paris during the Easter weekend."

Time stops. I don't hear the birds chirping or the sounds of spring coming from the open window. The walls of my throat tighten and cave inwards, cutting off my air supply. He's looking at me, but I don't meet his eyes.

"Perhaps you can go to Munich, visit Toby."

I nod.

He's going to see her.

Hot tears prick the back of my eyes, but I'm determined that they will not materialise.

"I'll call Toby," I manage to squeak out.

My voice sounds heavy in my ears.

I walk to the spare room to make the call, but it's

a while before I pick the phone up.

Standing by the window, a sensation I recognise as fear locks me in its powerful jaws.

'*He wants to keep you,*' the voice of reason reminds me, while fear reminds me that he loves another woman; the woman he's going to see. Images flash before my eyes. I want to hate him, but he did warn me.

I was foolish. I thought my heart was untouchable.

* * *

"Dylan?"

His voice breaks into my thoughts, "You haven't touched your supper."

I'd made pearl barley soup. It's my go-to meal whenever I'm feeling down, but I haven't eaten one drop. It sits on the table, turning cold. His bowl is empty as he had two portions with homemade bread and malt vinegar.

"I'm not hungry," the tears fall freely.

He's up in a flash, lifting me in his arms and taking

me to the couch. I sit on his lap and sob. A dam has burst, and my emotions pour out of me. I don't want him to go, but I don't know how to ask him to stay.

"Dylan, please talk to me. Tell me what you want. I'll do anything," he pleads.

I cannot resist when he speaks in this way. I adjust myself to sit astride him.

"No. Dylan. I don't think this will help you right now."

"Why are you going to Paris? Why can't you wait until she comes back to the UK?"

"When she comes back, it won't be to me. I need to let her know that."

"What about your feelings for her?"

"Dylan, I do love her, but sometimes it takes more than love to keep two people together."

"What's more than love?"

"You."

* * *

Choosing Me

I fly out on Good Friday. I travel light with only a small backpack. It's my first time travelling in first class. The lunch is served with real cutlery. It's grilled Salmon on a bed of creamy new potatoes and looks delicious...If only I could eat.

I replay last night in my head over and over. He'd offered to sleep in my spare bedroom, but it didn't take long for my resolve to break. I clung to him desperately and never want to feel that way again.

Toby meets me at the airport. I fall into his arms, and as usual, seeing my buddy restores some of my happiness. Munich is a beautiful city, and we spend the day walking the streets, taking it all in.

Toby tells me he works twenty-four-seven and is happy to take a break. We stay out all day, returning to his apartment well after midnight.

I'm freshly washed and, in my pyjamas, when I go to say goodnight.

"What can we do tomorrow?"

"I have a photoshoot. Work wants me to have some headshots done. I've booked a studio not far from here, but after that, I'm all yours."

I go along with him as I can't bear to be left alone.

When we arrive at the Foto studio von Herrn Nicolos, we are greeted by a young lady at the reception, who introduces herself as Ana. She takes us in. I relax and have fun as I watch the team prep Toby for his photoshoot.

My eyes are on Toby, so I see the moment it happens. I follow his gaze to the back of the room and notice a man with long, neat locks tied in a ponytail. He holds a camera as he approaches, and his presence lights up the room.

Ana passes him a cup of coffee, and he takes a sip before giving it back to her. He notices me and smiles, so I smile back.

"Hello, I'm Nicolos. Can I offer you a cappuccino?"

His English is impeccable though he speaks with a distinct German accent.

I introduce myself and tell him, "Yes, please."

Choosing Me

He turns to look at Toby, "You must be Tobias. Your girlfriend is very beautiful."

He shakes Toby's hand, and I see sparks fly.

"I'm not his girlfriend."

"She's not my girlfriend."

"I would love to take your photo," he says, his warm eyes appraising me.

"Toby is the model today, not me."

"Hmm," he says while he glances back at Toby; I take the opportunity to check him out.

He is of medium build with a smooth, clear, café au lait complexion. He's not as tall as Toby, but he is very attractive. He has broad shoulders and a slim waist, impeccably dressed too, and his crisp white shirt is tucked into fitted black jeans. I like him immediately. He flirts with me, but I can see right through it.

Toby cannot keep a straight face during the photoshoot.

"That's a wrap!" Nicolos says after ten minutes.

"Already? Are you sure?"

"Toby's face looks the same from all angles. This job is too easy," says Nicolos, "Now you, on the other hand, your face is interesting. Would you like to see?"

The tables are turned, and suddenly, I'm being prepped by the team and having my pictures taken.

"Kein make-up Ana bitte, naturlich," Nicolos says to Ana.

Toby comes alive in the studio, and I welcome the distraction from my worries. The chemistry between the two men is electric. Nicolos' team give each other knowing looks.

They congregate by the coffee machine, gossiping away, and I don't have to speak German to know what they're saying.

I spend the next hour having my photo taken from all angles. Toby makes suggestions as he knows my best looks.

I question Nicolos about his life. He's the youngest of three. His father is French and a university lecturer; his mother is African and a schoolteacher. He was born in Botswana, but his family moved to Hamburg when he was three. Yes, he's been to London several times.

He travels the world taking photographs of models, movie sets, and fashion shows, but his specialty is nature.

He freelances for *National Geographic*. I think to myself, if Toby is not sold on this guy, I'll have to take him for myself.

When Nicolos goes off to his dark room, Toby and I sit drinking coffee and snacking on dried fruit.

"You're such a natural D. The pictures will be beautiful."

He's not wrong. Nicolos shows us the photos, and I don't believe it's me. He surprises me by offering to pay me for my time, despite my protests, and he also gives me three photos free of charge.

All four of us go out to lunch. The fact that Nicolos brings his assistant along is not lost on me. I mostly chat with Ana at the restaurant. It's not easy, but I understand a few more German words by the end.

We eventually leave them to head out to enjoy the afternoon sunshine. We buy food from the stalls in the market and walk the rest of the day before returning to his place.

Toby is unusually quiet. I don't want to press him too much, but I'm curious to know if he'll call Nicolos. He tells me he has work to finish, so I leave him alone. I check my phone, and my mood nosedives when I have no missed calls or messages.

Hot tears prick my eyes, and I shut the phone and bury it deep in my bag. The walls creep closer, boxing me in. The air is close, and I struggle to pull oxygen in. The sensation causes my heart to race erratically, so I seek out Toby's company. He's standing outdoors on the balcony, staring intently at the fading sun, and I move closer, wrapping my arms around him.

His face mirrors the way I am feeling on the inside.

Choosing Me

"Toby, what's wrong?"

"I liked him."

I'm confused as to why this is a sad thing.

"He liked you too. It was obvious. He didn't want to take my photos. It was a ploy to be around you for longer."

He sighs, shielding his eyes from the orange glow of the evening skyline.

We watch in silence as the sun goes down and the darkness descends. Back inside, I make ginger tea, carefully placing the steaming mug on the table where he sits, seeming a little lost.

"What are you worried about?" I ask.

He shrugs, but I've been wondering about this for ages, so I persist, "Toby, tell me. I want to help."

He doesn't speak for a while, but then his shoulders shake, and I realise he's crying. I'm up in a flash, grabbing tissues and wiping his tears; my beautiful friend, who I love so much.

"I can't do it," he says.

"Do what?"

"Be with a man."

"You're not gay?"

He gazes up at me; his eyes are like liquid gold.

"I am," he says, "but it makes me sick."

I don't speak; I wait for him to explain. He sits hunched over, and it breaks my heart.

"I'm afraid to go through with it."

"Do you mean sex?"

"Yes."

"Do you know why you feel this way?"

"When I was fourteen, I was with another boy at my school. We were on the swim team together,"

His voice breaks as he speaks, and my heart sinks into the pit of my stomach.

"With Markus?"

My voice is barely a whisper, but Toby laughs out loud. It startles me as I was not expecting it.

Choosing Me

"I'm sorry, D, the look on your face is priceless."

I'd be happy to cheer him up any other day, but not right now.

"No. Not with Markus, but he did save me from drowning. He ah...beat me up... and then I hit my head and fell in the lake. Markus pulled me out,"

Toby's voice is heavy, and I'm not able to follow the story very well.

"Let me see if I understand. You were with another boy, and he beat you up? How does Markus fit into the story?"

Toby gazes at me and sighs.

"One of the senior boys, his name was Simon, he asked me to meet him after lights out. I don't know why I agreed. None of those boys liked me, but I was young and confused. I couldn't talk to anyone about how I was feeling. He just started kissing me, and I didn't question it, but he said some things after that I don't want to repeat. I don't know why Markus was there that night, but he saved my life when all I wanted to do was die," his voice fades, and I pull him closer, trying to take away his pain. I kiss his cheek.

"I'm so sorry that happened to you, but you have so much love to give, don't let one bad experience ruin your chance to be happy."

His eyes hold mine, hanging on to my words, then he wraps his arms around me, and I kiss the top of his head.

"Thank you for loving me," he says.

"Always."

"Markus is a very lucky man," he smiles through his tears, and shame consumes me.

"Toby, I know you think that Markus and I are together, but it's not like that. He loves someone else, and I feel guilty about my actions. I never should've started seeing him. Now it's one big mess."

"Nothing worth having is ever easy. Don't give up before you've even begun."

"He went to see her," my voice is soft.

"I know," he says.

I stare at him, "He told you?"

Choosing Me

The chambers of my heart threaten to burst through my chest.

"You're forgetting that he's my friend, and you're my beautiful girl. If he hurts you, he answers to me."

"Toby, he was honest with me from the start. It's not his fault. I just... didn't expect to feel this way about him. It will be hard to give him up, that's all."

"Haven't you figured it out yet? He's crazy about you."

"He seems conflicted. Being with him is amazing, but he *loves her.*"

"I probably shouldn't be telling you this. He loves her, but he is in love with you, and he has no intention of ever giving you up. He's waiting for you to sort through your feelings about him, but I think you already know."

"Waiting for me?"

"Yes."

"I think you should tell him how you feel."

"I'm afraid, Toby."

"I know…"

Choosing Me

Balancing

The raindrops on the window shimmer like tiny stars. I arrive back in London on a wet and rainy Easter Monday. As the plane descends and lands on the slick tarmac, my mood goes with it. I'm nervous as thoughts of Markus never leave my head. I replay my talk with Toby.

I don't delay; I retrieve my carry-on bag and race through Immigration. When I walk out of the terminal, he's there, waiting at the arrivals. My heart swells at the beautiful sight before me.

"My dreams didn't do you justice," he says, and pulls me into his arms.

The warmth spreads through my body like wildfire, so I wrap my arms around his neck and breathe him in. I don't realise I'm crying until he wipes my tears away. He takes my bag and reaches for my hand, leading the way out to the car park.

We're both quiet on the drive, and I steal glances at him.

He's more beautiful than I remember.

The radio plays softly, and the lush greenery blurs past the window. I always love coming home to London. It's how I know that it's really my home. I say this to him, and he reaches out to touch me briefly before pulling his hand back to change gears.

As we pull off the motorway, my heartbeat accelerates. I don't know if he plans to stay at my place. He switches off the engine, and I turn to him; there is so much I want to say.

"Thank you."

He smiles at me, "It was my pleasure."

He takes my hand in his; mine are cold, his are warm. I fleetingly wonder if this is what our hearts are like; his always warm and beating steadily, while mine, cold and erratic, like my ever-shifting moods.

He caresses my cheek with the back of his index finger, and we stare into each other's eyes. His appear soft and almost grey in the dreary weather. The smell of apples lingers in the car. The interior is glossy, with not a single dust mite visible.

A second passes before his mouth is on mine; a moan escapes my throat.

Were his kisses always this good?

"Do you want to come upstairs?"

"Yes, very much," he says, opening the car door.

The rain falls heavier still. I run to the door of my building, sheltering under the awning, waiting for him. He removes my bag and a bouquet of flowers from his boot; the rain is drenching the white hydrangeas.

"Thank you, they're so lovely," I say and open the

door.

The apartment is cold, so I switch on the heaters.

He is filling the vase in the spare room when I show up with just my towel wrapped around me. He walks toward me, slowly pulling his t-shirt over his head.

He removes his jeans, never taking his eyes off me. Our lips make contact, and we both react. Moaning in unison. He removes my towel, and his eyes feast on my body. He then lays me on the bed and lies next to me. I run my hand over his chest and down his torso; his abs are rippling at my touch. He closes his eyes and exhales sharply as my fingers explore, feeling my way over his naked body.

I am content to lie here next to him.

"I missed you," I whisper.

He rolls on top of me. His hard nakedness is against my soft, supple flesh. I imprint his face in my memory.

We should talk; there's much to say, but I want to

feel him buried deep inside me for now.

I wrap my legs around him to let him know I'm ready. My fingers grip the hard muscles of his butt as he slowly sinks into my slippery centre, and the sensation is so good; I know I'll never stop wanting him.

"Markus!" a strangled cry catches in my throat, and my tears start to flow.

He moves excruciatingly slowly, and I beg him to take me harder, faster.

"Just feel me, Dylan."

He pulls all the way out of my body, slick with desire, and slowly all the way in again. My body smoulders like a slow burn, threatening to erupt any minute.

It's too much.

"Please," I beg.

He answers my plea. He is quicker now, kissing me with urgency. My fingers grip him harder as he takes me higher than ever before.

The time's up for me. I'm at the edge, and he loves me deeper and faster. He pushes down on my core with his hand, his mouth on mine, tasting and sucking as I moan with pleasure, and then, he ignites. I let go seconds later with his name on my lips.

It's a few minutes before either of us can move. I listen to our breathing as we drift back to Earth. The room is now completely dark, apart from the strips of light coming from the hallway. Heavy rain persists, beating against the window. I could lie here with him forever, but my tummy rumbles, and he chuckles.

I've not eaten since I had breakfast with Toby earlier today. Reluctantly, I uncurl myself from our blissful coupling to satiate my other hunger.

If I only had to cater for myself, this would be easy. There is not much in the refrigerator, but the cupboards are stacked.

I make lentil soup and toast some bread. I have a non-dairy spread and one over-ripe avocado that is somehow still alright, so I add that to the mix. In the end, it's a very satisfying meal.

Choosing Me

* * *

I'm sitting on the bed, with my back against the headboard, and he sits facing me, with his hands on my bare legs.

The rain has eased, but the wind has picked up, howling, and rattling the shutters. I snuggle closer to him. The mood in the room has shifted.

"What happened in Paris?"

He doesn't answer at first, but I patiently wait for him.

"We both agreed to move on with our lives."

"Are you okay?"

"Yes."

I want to ask him why he is sad, but I remember they were together for sometime, and I let it be.

"I'm sorry," I say.

"It was the right thing to do. I kept putting it off for so long."

"Because you love her."

I turn my head towards the window, watching the trees bend and sway. He turns it back gently, so I can no longer avoid his eyes.

"No, I was worried about how she would react. She can become upset and emotional, which is never easy. I don't like hurting her."

"I guess she must have been quite upset."

It is a moment before he responds, "No, she wasn't. It was a bit unnerving. She was more resolved this time. Calm."

He plays with my fingers as he speaks.

"Did that bother you then? That she wasn't crying over the loss?"

He gazes into my eyes, "It means I'm free to make you promises and ask you to be mine, but I don't know if that's what you want."

I look down at our fingers entwined before meeting his gaze, "I do."

His face splits into the most breathtakingly beautiful smile. I'm stunned that I can evoke such joy in another human being with just two words.

I return his smile. He kisses me slowly at first, before moving with more urgency. His fingers are in my hair, which is spilling over my shoulders. He takes my hand and pulls me off the bed, so I'm standing between his legs. Goose bumps rise on my exposed flesh as he removes my sweater.

I close my eyes, wanting to absorb every sensation. He touches my body, but it's my soul that lights up. I open for him to enter; all my senses are heightened, and our joined bodies connect more intimately than our previous lovemaking.

He wipes my tears before I realise, I'm crying, then smiles and whispers my name.

I press my body to him, and he slides deeper within me. It shatters everything I thought I knew about being with someone. My heart explodes with fullness, swollen from this seismic shift, and the act of giving myself to him is climactic.

What I'm feeling is not yet clear to me, but I suspect this could be *love*.

Afterwards, he holds me, and I recount Toby's story of being beaten in the woods.

"Why didn't you tell me?"

I lie facing him, and he's lying on his back. He reaches over and pulls a blanket over me, and I place my hand on his stomach. He caresses my shoulder.

"When you asked if I'd seen him with other boys, I thought of it, but it's not really my story to tell. It happened to him, not me."

"He was so upset. I'd never seen him like that before. It was a bit of a shock,"

Tears pool in my eyes before spilling over, and he wipes them away.

"Why were you in the woods? Toby said it was midnight."

Markus doesn't respond for a while, and I suspect he doesn't want to say, so I don't press him. He sighs and looks into my eyes, so I give him a small smile to encourage him.

"It was a difficult time for me. We'd just returned

to school. At the end of the summer holiday my grandfather had told me he was dying. He was suffering from heart disease. I'm not sure why he told me, but I couldn't sleep, so I would wander in the woods at night. We camped a lot, Grandpa and I, so being in the woods helped me come to terms with it."

His voice trails off, and then he smiles sadly.

"I find it strange that Toby thinks I saved his life. When I think of that time, I remember my grandfather saving mine."

His voice is so full of emotion that I don't dare to interrupt him.

"I did see them together, Toby and Simon. It didn't register, though. I didn't feel anything seeing them kissing. I just kept walking, but then I heard the cries, so I ran back and saw Toby in the water. I pulled him out and ran for help. Although, it was the next day that really stuck with me. We were in the shower room, and Simon said to me, 'Now that fag is out of the way, you'll be the champion swimmer again.' That's when I lost it. I beat him up so bad he was unconscious, and I had to leave school."

He is whispering now, and a shiver trickles down my spine. Markus is usually so calm and composed, and I cannot imagine him going off like that. He rolls over to face me, holds me close and soothes me, for I must look terrified.

"What happened to Simon?"

"He was alright; needed a few stitches. I think he hit his head on the wall, but got off light. Considering that Toby was in the hospital for a few days."

"Your grandfather must have been so mad at you."

"That's the thing; he wasn't mad. He never asked me what had happened. I wanted to tell him, but he said he didn't need to know. Simon's parents pressed charges and a lawsuit. Lord Justice Mills' grandson brought disgrace to his family."

"I didn't feel shame until the moment we had to go back to school to resolve the issue. Grandpa came with me. He was so frail but was still able to climb those steps with his cane. He wouldn't even let me help him up the stairs, and when he walked into the room, everyone was in awe of him."

"I didn't know anything about what he'd accomplished in his life, but I saw it then. By the end of the meeting, Simon's parents, the school board, and even Simon himself were under his spell. I was reinstated at school and back on the swim team. It was like nothing had ever happened, but then, Grandpa had me removed from the swim team."

I wait, but he doesn't say more.

"Why?"

"I did hurt someone, so I had to be punished for my actions, and I understood that. That's when I started running instead. I trained the whole winter, and when the season started, I was ready."

We are both silent for a while.

"Thank you for telling me. I'm sorry you lost your grandpa when you were so young."

"It's okay. He took his time but sent me you."

I smile, and he pulls me closer. We're both

naked, and as our bodies touch, my breasts swell, and my nipples become erect. He looks at them and smiles, kisses me, and we're off again.

I slide on top of him. His hands are on my hips, keeping me steady as he guides into me. I adjust myself to take as much of him as I can manage. I'm sodden, but I can feel every inch of him. He's breathing harder as I ride him, and my moans are almost guttural.

"Dylan..."

He's looking at our bodies moving together, and I can tell he loves seeing me like this. I feel pressure on my hips as he pushes me down onto him. I open my legs wider, determined to take all of him inside me. This drives him wild, and he whispers my name over and over, his eyes wondrously gazing into mine as I ride faster.

I am close to the end much too soon. I try to hold on, but he tells me to let go as he releases inside me. I try to suppress my delight, but my sounds escape, and I moan through the pleasure. I know I'm loud, but I have no control.

Markus laughs and rolls me onto my side, kissing me; I'm spent. He cleans us up and then climbs back into bed, holding me close.

"My beautiful girl, you're amazing."

I close my eyes and fall asleep.

***

Markus and I spend every moment of our time together. It's easy to be with him, and I feel extremely fortunate. I'm amazed I can keep my work up to its usual standard, as he's always on my mind. I make plans for everything we can do together.

I create complex designs for his food and experiment with different flavours. We eat out at Nate's, and I pick up some tips. Markus says he did not realise he was hungry until he met me, and he always talks like that. We even finish each other's sentences.

I believe that in life, there should always be a perfect balance. One of the reasons I relish my different moods is that I feel like I'm fulfilling that quota.

When Markus and I have our first disagreement, it's deliberate on my part. He's always so calm and patient with me that it makes me nervous.

The opportunity presents itself one Thursday evening. As usual, he picks me up from Paul's salon, and we eat out close to his apartment in Canary Wharf. He wants me to come back to his place after, but I say no. When he asks me why not, I answer stroppily.

He lets it go and drives us back to my place. I feel bad for disappointing him, especially because he'd asked so nicely. The truth of the matter is, I've always wanted to live in London, and Markus' place is, as they say, a prime location with the best view. I'm reluctant to go there. I can't have the happiness barometer too high, as then, the fall back to earth might break all my bones.

He tries to make small- talk in the car, but I only give non-committal responses, so he gives up and

Choosing Me

turns on the radio. Jesus to a Child starts to play, and I forget myself and smile.

Whenever I hear this song – the way George Michael sings – I am transported to a place I long to go but have not yet been.

The next song to play is Bruce Hornsby's, 'That's Just the Way It Is'. I know I've lost the fight before it has even begun. Markus pays attention to the details.

I sing along as I absolutely love this song. He plays all my favourites. When I relent and ask him how, he tells me that he had a compilation made up just for me, seeing as we spend so much time in the car.

By the time we arrive at my place, I'm out of reasons to be stroppy with him. In fact, I'm hoping he will ravish me as soon as we walk through the door. I lean into him suggestively as we climb the stairs.

Once we're inside, he tells me that he needs to work. I'm derailed again. It's nine-thirty and way past my bedtime, so I go about my usual routine and then head to bed. I read for a while; we've finished The Hobbit and have now started on The Fellowship.

I must have dozed off, but I hear when he comes into the bedroom. We keep the door closed now, as my sexual noises have gone up in decibels, and it makes me a little uncomfortable when I meet my neighbour – I don't look her in the eyes anymore when I say hello.

Markus stands at the foot of my bed, observing me. His pants hang low on his hips, and he is shirtless with his defined shoulders on display. I go to him, and kneeling on my bed, I caress his torso and kiss his chest. He is aroused, but he doesn't touch me. I smile to entice him.

"Markus, touch me."

He caresses my face, and I sit back on my legs, bewildered.

"Dylan, why don't you want to come to my place?"

I exhale and tell him the truth.

"I'm scared. I worry we might be moving too fast. What if I come to your place with you and something happens? I just feel more in control when I'm here."

Choosing Me

I look down at my hands, and he sits next to me.

"I do understand your fears, but we decided to be a couple, and I want to share my life with you. I want you to move in with me."

I must look terrified as he puts his arm around me and kisses me on the side of my head.

"I'm not ready for that."

I know this for sure.

"What will I do with my apartment?"

I move out of his embrace; I can't think when he's so close to me.

"I can pay for you to end the lease early," he says, shrugging his shoulders.

"My apartment is not leased. This is my place. I own it."

He appears surprised, and I stare him down. I don't need to fabricate reasons to be angry now; I'm annoyed that he's so arrogant.

"Sorry, I just assumed..." he begins.

He puts his hand on my thigh, but I push it away.

"Well, you know what they say about assumptions. You should be moving in with me!"

"There's more room at my place."

This is true.

"When did you buy this place?"

"Six months ago. My sister and I sold our childhood home. Grams had left it to us. I tried to buy a place in London, but it was over my budget. Moving to Essex, I could have a bigger place for a fraction of London prices, and the commute is easy."

He's quiet. He reaches out to take my hand, but I don't pull away this time.

"Why don't we compromise? We can trade off and spend time in both places," he says.

"I suppose. It sounds like the grown-up thing to do."

"Whatever it takes to make you happy. I didn't think I could love someone like this, so now that I have you, I never want to let you go."

Choosing Me

His eyes blaze, and I don't dare to speak. He smiles and leans in to kiss me.

"I love you," he whispers.

"I love you too."

The words leave my lips, and I know they're true.

* * *

When I finish work on Friday, Markus is waiting to take me to his place. There's no traffic, and all the lights are green as if to prove his point, so we arrive in fifteen minutes. The security gate is already open, so he drives straight through and parks the car.

Sunlight flashes like diamonds sparkling on the water, and a cool breeze flows in from the river.

The atmosphere is exuberant, with chic restaurants and bars lining the road just outside the gates.

Markus removes my bag from the boot and comes to take my hand. I try to act like nothing has impressed me so far, but it's very difficult. Right here is the London vibe I love, with the beautiful backdrop to make it irresistible.

He takes me over to the security desk to make a big show and dance about my arrival to the team. They issue me with the key card he must have pre-ordered, and I sign for it. When we're in the lift, I ask him about the stairs.

"They're through the sliding doors. I must caution you as we live on the top floor, so I'd say about a hundred and fifty steps, give or take."

"No problem for me. I can work out my thighs."

His eyes flicker to my legs. My dress comes to my mid-thigh, and my heels are high as usual. He doesn't say anything, but the look in his eyes is loaded with innuendos.

We enter his apartment. The sunlight shines through the tall glass windows, and the light touches everything. It's like walking into another world. Markus takes my bag upstairs and leaves me to look around. I watch him retreat, knowing that all his moves are calculated.

He wants me to like his place, but what's not to

like?

I remove my shoes and carry them as I walk through the lounge and into the kitchen area, and I don't touch anything.

The kitchen is triple the size of my tiny one. *Ridiculous*, I think, when he doesn't even cook. There are state-of-the-art buttons with gadgets. All the appliances are neatly tucked away, and the marble top gleams in the sunlight.

I notice there are yellow daffodils in vases around the apartment. I move away from the kitchen and go around the island towards the back of the apartment, and my heart almost stops.

The sight before me is truly spectacular. The balcony overlooks the Thames, and floor-to-ceiling glass walls showcase a panoramic view of the Dockland skyline.

"Wow!" I find my voice.

This apartment trumps mine.

Canary Place

"It pales in comparison to you," he whispers in my ear.

His sudden appearance makes me jump. He removes my shoes from my hands; I didn't realise I was still holding on to them.

"Let me take you on a tour. There's a cloakroom by the entrance, and next to it is the utility room."

I follow him up the stairs.

"There are two bedrooms, each with an ensuite."

The bedrooms are quite large and spacious.

"Which room is yours?"

He takes me into the larger of the two rooms; the walk-in wardrobe is twice the size of mine. The bedrooms have floor-to-ceiling glass walls, and I stare out into the cloudless sky.

At the end of the hallway, we go up a few steps, and he uses a key to open the door, and then we step outside.

"This is the best part. They've created this beautiful sky garden."

The garden is mostly green but is sprinkled with colourful spring flowers in full bloom. Hyacinth and daffodils perfume the air. The space is designed for entertaining or relaxing, and stylish furniture completes the look. There are wooden benches with white cushions, and a large white parasol sits in the centre of an oval dining table surrounded by four chairs.

"Do you want to go out to eat, or shall we order in?"

I shrug my shoulders and move away from him to sit on a wooden bench in the middle of the garden. Markus, sensing my mood, leaves me to myself. The sun feels nice, and I hold my face up, closing my eyes. I sit here until the sun goes down, and he comes to tell me that the dinner has arrived.

I remove my jacket and cardigan in front of the mirror, back inside the bedroom. My dress is strapless and reveals a lot of cleavage. I stare at the King-sized bed, suddenly feeling minuscule in his grand apartment.

He has set two places downstairs at his breakfast bar.

"Is it okay if we eat here?"

I think of the rooftop dining area and glance over at the solid oak table off to the side of the lounge area.

"Sure."

He pulls out one of the tall stool-type chairs and assists me as I sit. Up close, the marble worktop is stunning as it's embedded with tiny stars that appear to glitter under the lights.

"Nice dress."

"I've had this on all day."

"Have you?"

Typical, I think. *He only notices the dress now that I'm no longer wearing the cardigan, for obvious reasons.*

He's opening the food packets.

"It smells familiar. Have we had this before?"

"It's from Bombay in Shoreditch. Remember, we went there."

I know he means the first day I kissed him seven weeks ago. We look at each other and smile. He indicates for me to eat, and I start digging in.

"So, what do you think?" he asks.

"It tastes much better than last time," I say, spooning more into my mouth.

He laughs, "I meant the apartment."

"I love it."

He smiles happily. I'm learning how to read him;

his face gives nothing away as usual, but I can pick up on his body language, and occasionally, his eyes.

"Who takes care of the place when you're not here? The garden, the flowers?"

"I have a gardener. He takes care of the plants and maintains the sky garden. The cleaner comes twice a week. I asked her to put out flowers from the garden. I thought you'd like that."

He carries on eating, and I notice he also has a glass of wine, but I stick with my lemon water.

"Markus, I don't feel comfortable having a cleaner and a gardener. Strangers having access to the place where I live; It's a bit unnerving. I can clean myself and take care of the garden."

I know nothing about gardening, but how hard can it be?

He stops eating and stares at me, "Dylan, if I let them go, I'm putting two people out of a job that they do very well."

I suddenly feel foolish.

Choosing Me

"Good point. I guess I didn't think about that. Sorry."

I shut my mouth and eat my dinner. Afterwards, I happily tidy up.

He shows me around the neighbourhood, and I'm buzzing with excitement. We walk along the riverfront all the way down to the pier. There are buses heading for Greenwich, where Toby lives. He's coming home tomorrow, and we'll meet up to celebrate his news.

"I can take one bus from here to Toby's house."

"You can take the car," he offers.

"Toby and I can go to Sunday Market again. I miss that so much."

I am practically bouncing along the walkway.

"Not next Sunday, Dylan. I have plans."

"Oh, you don't have to come with us."

I'm smiling as I say this, and I kiss his hand. He stops walking and watches me.

"My parents are having a dinner party, and I was

hoping you'd come with me."

I release his hand and exhale softly.

"I thought we'd agreed to take things slowly. I'm not ready for that," my voice breaks a little.

"I understand. I promise this is not to rush you. It's just that it's my birthday next week, so I wanted you to be there."

"It's your birthday?"

Okay, he has got to stop doing this.

"Yes, May eighteenth."

"That's next Thursday. I've nothing to give you, so I guess I'll go shopping tomorrow."

"Dylan, you don't have to do that. Everything I want is standing right here in front of me."

I walk into his waiting arms. I cannot fathom how "just me" is enough for him. However, much later that evening, as I'm wrapped in his loving arms, spent and breathless, I become a true believer. The two-hour walk earlier only seems to have energised him. I'm going to have to start exercising regularly to build up my stamina if I want to keep up with my man.

I sleep until eleven the next morning. Markus has pulled the blinds down to keep out the light. I shower and dress, as I'm going shopping for a birthday gift.

He's sitting at the breakfast bar; his laptop is open on the marble top, and he appears to be reading. I stop and wonder if I should go into the kitchen as I don't want to disturb him. He turns, notices me and smiles while walking towards me.

"Good morning, nice sleep?" he kisses me.

"Yes, very nice."

It feels strange being at his place.

"Hungry?"

He takes me over to the kitchen. There's a box of pastries on the counter.

"Do you have oats?"

"There should be some in here. Just help yourself to whatever you like,"

He kisses me again and goes back to his reading. I try to be as quiet as possible and decide to eat my porridge on the balcony, as it's a nice sunny day. I ponder what to buy him for his birthday as I eat.

We've moved so fast into this relationship and barely know each other. He is going to be twenty-seven. I recall him saying this to me on the first night we met. I'm already stressed, and it's only midday.

I tidy up the kitchen and tell Markus that I'm heading out, but I don't wait for a response. I kiss him and go out the door.

I feel free as soon as I'm outside. The London vibe is on full display, and I am in my element. I jump on the tube and head to Oxford Circus. I buy Toby a coffee mug that says "BOSS"; I know he'll like that.

I buy myself lingerie, workout clothes and new running shoes. I have my toenails painted in pink blush, which is a nice spring colour.

My feet are overheating in my boots, so I buy sandals and change into them. I sit at a small café and sip tea seeped in fresh mint leaves and people-watch for a while. I've been out for over three hours and have still not bought anything for Markus.

Choosing Me

My phone rings. I check the ID and smile.

"Toby!"

"Hello, D!" he says, "Markus said you're out shopping. Without me! How could you?"

His voice sounds good.

"Markus tells me it's his birthday, Toby, and I have no idea what to get him."

"Let me guess, you bought yourself something new," he says.

He knows me so well.

"I don't want to waste the trip completely, do I?"

He chuckles.

"D, I missed you," he says.

"Are you home?"

"Yes, just arrived a few minutes ago. I had a message from Markus. He sent me the address for the venue tonight. We're meeting up at six thirty."

"In that case, I'm going to head back now so I can get ready."

We say goodbye, and I hail a black taxi. Markus greets me at the door, pulling me in for a kiss. My bags fall to the floor as the kiss deepens. He grabs my butt and lifts me up. I can feel his welcome greeting through my thin skirt.

I laugh and pull away, and he helps me collect my things. He asks about my day as I remove my sandals and go up the stairs to put the clothes away.

I undress, and he follows me into the ensuite. There are large mirrors all around with neutral shade tiles. The bathroom does not have a bathtub. He leans against the door, his arms folded, and watches as I pin my hair up. I catch his movement in the mirror.

"Markus, No. Don't even think about it."

He helps me pin my hair up and smiles at me in the mirror. I grab the shower cap, turning the water on full force; It's nice and hot. I clean my body while he stands watching. He has an intense stare that I'm used to, and it turns me on.

I switch off the shower and open the door. He holds out a towel and wraps it around me, then takes

Choosing Me

my hand and leads me to his bedroom.

He dries my body and rubs moisturiser onto my skin. His attention to detail amazes me yet again. He lingers on my breasts, rubbing and kneading, carefully working his way down my body to my legs, and I close my eyes, exhaling sharply. He moves to my back, gently massaging the muscles of my derriere.

My moans of pleasure escape as heat pools in my core like molten lava. He falls to his knees, and although I know what will come next, I still cry out. He kisses my inner thigh and teases me with his fingers.

My legs tremble uncontrollably. His fingers open me wider, his tongue touches my innermost core, and I detonate, falling over.

He catches me in his lap on the floor. I'm whimpering, so he holds me close and soothes me. I still have the shower cap on, so he removes it and takes out the pins from my hair. He runs his fingers through, combing out the tresses, and continues to soothe me until I am calm again. He smiles and bends to whisper.

"The beauty of this place is that you can be as loud as you want. The walls are soundproof."

I stare at his swollen lips when he speaks. I trace them with my fingers and kiss him.

"Thank you," I croak.

"My pleasure."

* * *

We walk into Nate's restaurant hand-in-hand, and I receive my second surprise of the evening. Toby sits at the bar, and next to him is Nicolos wearing a leather jacket, oozing charm, and sex appeal. Toby spots us first, and we greet them both warmly.

I introduce Markus to Nicolos as my boyfriend, and Toby closes his eyes and smiles. I doubt he thought those words would ever be uttered from my mouth. He gives me another squeeze, and we go over to order drinks from the bar.

There is a Caribbean ambience in the restaurant tonight. A live band plays Soca music, and it takes me back to carnival seasons on the road with daddy and Kizzy. My father's band played on the Caribbean Islands of Grenada, St Vincent, Tortola, and Montserrat and then moved on to the Florida Keys. Those were fun times. My dad's bandmates used to look out for us as if we were their own children.

I order a virgin colada. The bartender serves my drink with a wink, and I smile. I tell Markus that it's completely vegan but with no alcohol. I offer him a sip, and he orders one for himself with alcohol.

I sing along to the songs I recognise. The bass player notices me and serenades me with a solo piece, so I give him a round of applause. Markus stares when I go back to the bar, and I smile at him.

He pulls me into his arms, and I wrap mine around him, kissing his cheek. The men chat away, but I'm absorbed in the music. When the band takes a break, Markus asks how I know the songs, and I tell him about my dad's band.

"There's so much we don't know about each other," I say.

Are we crazy to build this relationship on such limited knowledge?

"The more I know about you, the more I love you. You're everything I've ever wanted in a woman. We'll just figure out the rest as we go along."

He kisses me, and I taste the alcohol on his lips. We head upstairs for dinner. Nate is not here tonight, but his head chef caters to us. We have the entire restaurant to ourselves, and I wonder how Markus has pulled this off. I'm in a nostalgic mood, so I order lamb stew. I occasionally catch Toby's eye, and we smile at each other.

I cuddle up to my bestie later in the evening. He rubs my arm, and I put my head on his shoulder.

"You and Markus look like a bona fide couple."

"What about you and Nicolos? He seems so into you, but who can resist your charms."

Toby glances over at Nicolos sitting at the bar chatting with Markus.

"Nicolos is very comfortable in his own skin. He doesn't hide who he is, whereas I've been closeted for

Choosing Me

most of my life. It's harder."

I squeeze his hand, and he kisses my hair the way Markus usually does.

"You're having fun, right?"

"Yes. He's amazing," his face splits into a huge grin.

"And he came all this way just to be here with you tonight, so I'd say he's a keeper."

* * *

Markus is slightly tipsy when I help him out of the cab. He leans on me, and I take him upstairs and help him to bed.

I watch him as he sleeps, and a sensation akin to panic starts to rumble deep in my belly. I have no clue how to make this relationship work.

Apart from the one Grams and Papa Kit had, I don't know of any relationships that have survived. I think of my parents' heart-breaking ending — how my father never got over my mother — and the fear bubbles inside me.

I sigh heavily. The one thing I've always done in my life is to stay true to myself. I decide to stick with this formula as it hasn't failed me yet, but it is all I know.

The next morning, I meet Toby at his place after borrowing Markus' car, and we drive to Walthamstow Farmers Market in the east end of London. We avoid discussing the men in our lives to reclaim our playful mood. It's a good call, as we're more relaxed. Toby turns the radio up, and we sing along as the car cruises down the north circular road.

We buy fresh produce at the market.

"It's time to see what that fancy kitchen has to offer," I say.

We don't linger, as Toby has his big day tomorrow. My vegan recipe books are back at my place, so I make a detour to collect them. The pictures from Nicolos are still in my apartment, one of which will be Markus' birthday gift, and Toby will contribute with a bottle of Merlot.

I drop him back at his place just after two p.m.

Choosing Me

Usually, we would go back to his place or mine, depending on which market we went to. Today, we would've been back at my place in Essex. We would cook, relax, and eat. For the past year, this has been my refuge.

Toby reassures me in the car, "D, we'll do our thing again. Tomorrow is going to be crazy as I have so much to do."

He's right. He's officially the CFO from tomorrow. Toby is only twenty-seven years old, but he was always going to be a high achiever.

"I know. I'm proud of you."

He kisses me goodbye, and I drive back to Markus. I find him sitting at his table with his laptop open. I stop and stare at him. He's wearing glasses. He removes them and comes over to greet me.

"Hey gorgeous," he offers me a kiss.

"Hey," I smile at him.

When I left this morning, he was still in bed after his night of drinking. He only groaned when I said I was off, but he's fully awake now.

"Do you wear glasses?"

"I don't need them all the time, just when my eyes are tired, and consuming copious amounts of alcohol does not help."

"Can you wear them to bed tonight? You look sexy."

He laughs, and we spend a few minutes reacquainting. My shopping bags are in the car, and I make several trips to retrieve them. Markus offers to help, but I decline, and he goes back to his reading.

We sit down to eat a few hours later. Dinner consists of leek and mushroom pie, with a large garden salad filled with avocado and olives. For dessert, we have apple and rhubarb crumble. He digs in, complimenting my culinary skills as usual.

"Dylan. This is amazing."

"Thanks. Your kitchen is officially broken in. No longer a virgin."

"You should try some of this," he says, referring

to the pie.

I had only served myself the salad.

"Dylan, you don't eat very much."

"I know I should eat more, but I worry about gaining weight. I'm sure I've gained weight just by making that pie."

"You can come running with me."

"Markus, I can't keep up with you in bed. How can I go running with you?"

"I would run with you. You can go at your pace."

"That won't be much fun for you."

"It is."

After dinner, he tells me to sit and relax while he cleans the kitchen. I sit at the breakfast bar watching him. His actions are mechanical as he wipes the stove and all the cupboard doors. I didn't notice it before because we were always at my place, but now it's so obvious.

"OCD much?"

"Actually, I'm being meticulous, as I know that's how you like things."

"Hey, I can admit I'm slightly neurotic, but you're in denial."

He sits on the stool next to me and runs his fingers along my midriff. The setting sun illuminates the room, and his eyes turn to burnt copper.

My eyes cast downwards as it's terrifying for me to see the intense look in his eyes, but he comes closer and kisses me tenderly. I can almost believe this is possible. He wraps his arms around me, and his warmth radiates through my body. The feeling consumes me. I want to move away, but he holds me close.

* * *

"Dylan, I won't be able to meet you for lunch today."

It's Monday morning, and I'm making a salad for lunch in the kitchen.

I didn't realise he expected to meet for lunch. I

mean, we live together now, and Toby's back.

"Busy day today?"

"I'm behind with a few deadlines at work."

"How come?"

"I've been spending all my time trying to woo you."

"I'll work late for a couple of nights this week as I have the day off on Thursday," he adds.

I'm about to ask why when I remember it's his birthday.

"What do you want to do for your birthday?"

"We're going to Savannah's place."

He goes around the island to put his dish in the dishwasher, then heads upstairs.

"Sarah is coming today, Dylan, so no need to wash up."

I think Sarah must be the cleaner, but Savannah is a mystery; perhaps she is his sister. It dawns on me that I must be in love with the sex, as I have no clue about this man's life. He appears to be in a hurry today, so I finish up and grab my bag.

"Savannah is your sister?" I ask as he locks up, and we head out of the apartment and into the lift.

"Yes, of course," he replies as if I should know this.

He holds the car door open for me, and I buckle my seatbelt.

"So, we're going to see your family on Thursday now, not Sunday?"

"No, we're going to my sister's house. We always celebrate the actual day together if we can. Then, on Sunday, my parents are having a dinner party for us."

He drives through the gate and carefully pulls out into the street, which is busy with pedestrians.

"Your sister is throwing you a party?"

"I think we're going out for a meal."

My confusion must be evident because he suddenly says, "It's her birthday too; we're twins. Sorry, Dylan, I thought I mentioned this."

Choosing Me

He pulls up outside my building, and I'm tempted to slam the car door, but he comes around to open it for me. He escorts me across the road and walks me into the reception area, holding my hand.

We arrive extra early today, so I have a few minutes to kill anyway. I exhale, ready to admonish him for his lack of information, but he disarms me with his usual charm.

"Dylan, thank you for an amazing weekend."

He's smiling, and of course, I'm now grinning like a Cheshire cat.

***

I'm called into my new boss' office at eleven a.m. I leave my desk with his gift in hand. His office is on the very top floor, and I take the stairs instead of the lift. The name on the door says "Tobias Smith, CFO". I open the door and go in. I'm a little out of breath. There are others in the room, so I find the only empty chair.

Toby is sitting at his desk; he smiles at me and then addresses the room. He has a presentation slide with his strategy for the next year.

The plan highlights what we do well and the areas we need to improve. The focus will be on staff training and retaining key personnel. I look around the room, and everyone seems interested in what he is saying.

The meeting lasts only fifteen minutes. He then asks if anyone has questions before everyone is dismissed. A lady called Jane asks me to stay back after everyone else has left. Toby tells me Jane is going to be his new assistant, shadowing his role. I smile as I think it's a good choice.

Toby is rewarding loyal staff members rather than employing new people. Jane used to work with Toby in corporate finance. He tells me I'll be taking Jane's old role and can start training this afternoon. I'll be moving to the corporate team.

I'm stunned. I think people will say it's because Toby and I are close, but I thank them both and walk out before realising I still have his gift. I walk back into the office, and both of them look up at me. I put the gift on Toby's desk and smile apologetically before leaving quietly. While pulling the door closed, I catch Toby's eye, and he winks at me.

Birthday Surprise

Markus is working late again this evening. Today was another busy day, so I didn't notice his text messages until late afternoon, telling me he could not pick me up as he was meeting a client for dinner. I didn't have time to stop for lunch.

I hail a taxi to take me back to Canary Place.

Just as I put the cake mix into the oven, Toby calls, and we chat for a bit. He apologises for missing lunch today, as he'd been meeting customers. I tell him it's okay and that we still have Sunday Market.

"Enjoy your day off tomorrow, D."

The aroma of the cake fills the air as I leave it to cool on the side. I miss my place; this penthouse in the sky eclipses my tiny apartment, but it feels cold and empty when Markus is not here.

It takes me a moment before I figure out all the buttons on his fancy stereo, but soon, the soulful sound of Luther fills the air. I pull out my Blackberry and make a note of Markus' birthday in my calendar. Just in case we're still together next year, I think darkly.

A reminder flashes up for my appointment with the gynaecologist next week. We need to sort out better contraception as we've not been using condoms much.

I'm sitting on the couch, wrapped in a blanket, and reading when he arrives. My heart skips a beat when I see him, and my melancholy disappears.

He runs up the stairs to shower and change, and then he comes to join me on the couch.

His eyes tell me what he has on his mind, but I have other ideas.

"Can we talk?" My voice is soft.

"Sure, how was your day?"

"Who am I meeting from your family?"

"My sister, Savannah. She lives in Belsize Park with her Border Terrier Bruno; he hates me by the way, which is the only reason she picked him."

"On Sunday, you'll meet my parents, my mother, Helen, and dad, Matthew. They live in Wimbledon Village. They may have invited my aunt Connie and her husband Rob, possibly my cousins Josh and Holly, but I don't know. You'll also meet Becca; she lives with my parents."

"Okay, thanks."

"What about you, Dylan? You never seem to want to talk about your family."

"It's not the fairy-tale family that you have."

He lifts my head gently and kisses me softly.

"Tell me."

Choosing Me

"You already know some of it. My sister and I were raised by our grandparents, Rosemary, and Christopher. We grew up in Plymouth, Massachusetts. We went to live with them when I was six and my sister was four because my dad couldn't manage two young girls as he made his living on the road. Papa Kit died when I was sixteen, and my Grams passed almost two years ago."

I'm hoping this is enough information for him.

"What about your mother?"

He asks the one thing I don't want him to.

"You mentioned she was unwell. Is that why she couldn't take care of you and your sister? What's your sister's name?"

"Kizzy."

"Why could she not look after you and Kizzy?"

"Postpartum, I think. It's the only explanation I have."

"Why do you think that?"

"Well, because Kizzy was left in the hospital. My

mom gave birth to her and then left."

"I'm so sorry. How old were you?"

"I was almost two years old and even though I was so young it was like I knew the instant she was gone. I would spend hours looking out the window, waiting for her to come back."

I go to the cloakroom, take a picture from my wallet, and show it to Markus. In the picture, my mom is wearing a sleeveless white dress, and I'm tiny in her arms. It was the day of my christening.

"Wow. Dylan, this is you."

"Well, yes. I'm the baby in the photo."

He smiles.

"She's beautiful. She looks quite young."

"She's eighteen in the picture. She was three months pregnant with me when she married Daddy. Some of the photos used to upset me so he locked them away. But he allowed me to keep this one. I never show it to anyone, I'm too afraid Kizzy will find out that I have it."

Choosing Me

He passes it back to me. I put the picture back in my wallet, then walk into his outstretched arms.

"Thank you for telling me. I understand why you don't like to talk about it."

He strokes my hair; his voice is soothing.

"Where did the book go?"

He reaches over to the sideboard and passes it to me.

"Read to me?"

He opens the novel to our last page and starts to read.

* * *

"Happy Birthday!"

"Dylan, you look beautiful."

My new silk negligee spills all around me as I climb on top of him, and he grabs my hips. I am naked underneath. The birthday boy is ever ready, and my core stretches to accommodate him. He closes his eyes and groans softly.

I begin a slow grind when he opens his eyes, gazing with emotion. He breathes deeper as his eyes drink me in. The thin straps of my gown have fallen down my shoulders. The white bodice clings to my breasts, and my hard nipples are visible through the thin, silky material.

The morning sunlight shines through the window and illuminates my skin. I could not have planned this moment better. He moves to kiss me, but I push him back down.

This is my rodeo.

When he caresses the exposed flesh of my derriere, I increase the tempo with my hands splayed on his chest.

I close my eyes and throw my head back, revelling in this sexy and powerful feeling. I move my hand up and down his stomach, and he erupts. Seconds later, I follow. I'm euphoric with my triumph as it was the first time, I rode him all the way to the finish.

I'm lying on top of him, recovering, and his fingers stroke my back.

Choosing Me

"I love you," he whispers.

"I love sex with you," I say, and he laughs.

"Shower with me."

Usually, I'd say no, but as it's his special day, I nod and smile. He lifts me off the bed and carries me to the bathroom before I can change my mind.

* * *

Markus pulls up outside a row of white townhouses. He parks the car behind a dark green Jaguar. Tall oak trees line the street, creating a lovely breeze. There is a beautiful rose garden in the square out front. This is, quite simply, a beautiful place to live.

I step out of the car and look up at the sky. The sun is shining, but storm clouds in the distance threaten rain. The boot slides open, and I remove my bag. My fingers tremble as I pull the strap over my head. We have arrived at Savannah's place, and it is just past noon.

He and I had a great morning together; he is in

such good spirits. I let him make love to me in the shower for the first time, and he took full advantage. Prior to that, my hair was beautiful and straight. It is now slicked back in a bun. There was no way to avoid getting it wet, so I salvaged my look as best as possible.

He said it would be an informal affair as we're only heading to see his sister, so I dress in black skinny jeans and a sleeveless, black pussy bow blouse with red love hearts.

I didn't want to go overboard with my look, but I still wanted to look nice; I can tell she's important to him.

He tells me this is the house, and I go up the steps. Looking back, I see him leaning against the car and grinning at me.

"What?" I ask, thinking this is the wrong house.

He runs up the steps and kisses me quickly on my lips.

"Just admiring the view," he replies with his hands on my hips.

I blush.

This is not the time for jokes; I'm already a bag of nerves.

He opens the door with a key, takes my hand, and then we go in. I've always had a preconceived notion that if someone lives in a place like this, they could only be one type: posh, upper class and snooty, but Savannah surprises me. She's standing in her lounge and talking on the phone when we walk in.

"It's not rocket science, Graham, so try to make it happen without costing me the Earth."

Her accent is exactly like Markus', but her voice is sultry. Her long brown hair is piled on her head in a messy bun. She is tall and slender, like her brother. She turns to see us and smiles. I notice that she, too, has his smile.

"Graham, I've got to go now, but you can brief me tomorrow when I'm in the office," she hangs up the phone and hugs her brother.

"Markus, happy birthday, darling. How are you?"

"Happy birthday Vana. I'm good," he holds his sister in his arms and kisses her forehead.

She turns to me and pulls me into a hug.

"Dylan, it's nice to finally meet you."

"Happy birthday," I say shyly.

She stares at me then, and I swear, it's the same intense look that her brother has. She's the female version of him and very pretty. She has the same slightly tanned complexion.

"Markus did not exaggerate for the first time in his life. You're very beautiful."

"Thank you."

"Vana, when have I ever exaggerated in my life?"

"All the time, darling. I just don't always point it out."

She leads the way up the stairs. The layout of her place is interesting. The first thing I see is a long hallway leading to a mature garden. A winding staircase faces it, and her lounge is to the left. It's a grand room, complete with a fireplace. All the furniture is white, and on the right is an equally stunning dining area with an impressive chandelier.

I can't believe how spacious this place is. Her kitchen is at the very top of the house. It's cosy and inviting, with a large stone fireplace.

On the wall is a painting of a woman with dark cocoa skin; "DR Grace Luna Tambo" is written in bold gold letters under the image. I try not to stare. There are African artefacts on the walls and a picture of a vineyard from which Markus stares out as a young teenager.

His sister is standing next to him in the photograph. I want to take a closer look but don't want to appear nosy.

I can tell Savannah spends most of her time in this room. A low growling sound alarms me.

"Bruno, it's his birthday today. Be nice!"

The cutest little dog pokes his head up and comes over to us.

"Bruno hates Markus," Savannah tells me, and I

laugh.

There's a small leather couch in the kitchen, and Markus pulls me down to sit. Savannah is making us tea.

"Markus, you'll have to have it black. I don't have any of that nasty milk you like."

"I didn't expect you to make any special efforts today of all days, Vana."

Bruno lays down next to my feet. His fur is shiny, and I run my fingers along his back, which he seems to like because he settles down and grunts contentedly.

"Isn't he supposed to be aggressive towards strangers?"

Bruno puts his head up and barks at Markus.

"Don't antagonise him. Bruno is also welcoming if a guest is welcome in my home."

"So, I'm not welcome?"

"You're an exception to the rule, darling."

Savannah brings over the tea, places it on a coffee

table, pulls up a footstool and sits.

"Vana, I'll sit there. You sit on the couch."

They swap seats. Savannah has the same colour eyes as Markus, but hers are more stunning, with her incredibly long lashes.

"I'm taking you both to Martinelli's. We have a reservation for two o'clock. Hope that's okay."

"Is that a French restaurant?"

"They know how to cater for Markus, and we've been there a few times."

Bruno barks, and the doorbell chimes. Savannah excuses herself and rushes off to answer it. Markus takes the opportunity to sit next to me so we can kiss, but Bruno starts to growl, so Markus goes back to his stool.

"What did you do to him?"

"I've done nothing. He's hated me from day one."

"Markus, what have you done?" Savannah comes into the room, looking at him in disbelief.

She walks over and gives him a hug.

"What will daddy say?"

She sits next to me on the couch holding her brother's hand.

"He already knows, and he agrees with me. You're ready."

She looks over at my puzzled face and passes me an apostilled certificate. It mentions her name and eighty per cent shares, so I suspect he bought her shares in a company called Estonia Mills Ltd.

"It's our property business. Our family owns it. Markus has made me the majority shareholder by giving me another thirty per cent."

"What did you get me, Vana?"

"A case of wine from Dangote."

Markus laughs boyishly. Savannah goes off to freshen up.

"I didn't realise that you had a family business."

"Savannah is the one running the show, so it's only fair she should have control."

I learn something new about him every day. He

has a faraway look in his eyes. I interpret this to mean that he's not saying everything, but I don't press him to tell me.

***

We are treated to a late three-course lunch at the restaurant. The high street, just around the corner from Savannah's place, is lined with the best fine-dining restaurants. Savannah tells me she doesn't cook, and I tell her I know one other person who never cooks.

"It's never too late to learn new things. Dylan, perhaps you'll be kind enough to give me some cooking lessons."

"It would be my pleasure."

Being with Markus and his sister is so much fun; I completely relax and enjoy myself. Markus holds my hand and kisses me in a public display of affection. It feels natural, and it's his birthday, so I let him have his fun. He goes to the gents just before we're ready to leave.

"Just so you know, my brother is completely

altered. I've never seen him like this before. He's madly in love with you."

My laughter sounds nervous, "I feel as though Markus and I are in a speeding car with no brakes, going downhill. I just hope we have what it takes to survive."

"You will."

It starts to rain quite heavily as we walk back to Savannah's house. Markus holds a large umbrella over him and me, and we laugh as we walk, huddled together. Savannah is slightly ahead of us with her own umbrella.

As we approach the house, I notice an elegantly dressed woman standing at the door. She descends the steps as though she is about to leave. Then, before she crosses the street, she sees us and stops.

She doesn't have an umbrella, and her white coat is getting soaked. Her hair is already saturated.

"Stacey?"

Savannah walks back to us and gives Markus her

umbrella. I then watch him walk over to the woman and put the umbrella over her.

"Hello, Markus," her accent is British with a French lilt.

"You're soaked. Let's get you inside."

He helps her up the steps. Once we're all inside the kitchen, he takes off her coat. Savannah brings a warm blanket and towels for the woman to dry her hair.

She stands by the fireplace dripping on the tiles as Markus lights the fire. Then, he dries her hair, wraps the blanket around her, and makes her tea. I sit on the leather couch, watching them.

Savannah takes the wet towels away. The colour is coming back into the woman's cheeks, but her skin is like porcelain. The light from the fireplace dances across her face, giving her a mysterious look. Markus sits on the footstool next to her, while Savannah brings me a cup of tea and sits beside me on the couch. No one speaks. I assume we're all waiting for her.

Markus never mentioned her name to me, but I know it's her.

Stacey, he called her.

She looks over at me, and I don't look away. She has long, wavy, auburn hair, and a heart-shaped face with wide eyes. She wears a sleeveless white fitted top tucked into flared pants. She is very slim and very attractive.

"This is Dylan," says Markus when he notices her staring.

"Hello, Dylan," her voice is husky, and she speaks softly.

"Hi," this is all I can manage.

"Why are you here?" Markus finally asks now that she's no longer trembling and is warm.

"I'm so sorry to intrude on you like this. I knew you'd be here today. Happy birthday to you both," she says, smiling at Savannah.

"Thank you, Stacey," Savannah replies.

"You could have called me," says Markus.

Choosing Me

He seems annoyed, but she looks back at him with those beautiful eyes.

"I wanted to see you in person. There's something I need to tell you. Can we talk?"

She looks over at me and then back at him.

"Whatever you have to say, just say it. Dylan and I are together."

She hesitates, as if unsure, but then appears to decide.

"I'm pregnant."

Markus does not speak for a moment, then he says, "Okay," and shrugs his shoulders.

She lowers her voice further still, "It's yours."

Markus stands quickly, as if she has burned him, and glares down at her.

"What?" his voice is low, but a chill runs down my spine.

"How can this be, Stacey?" his voice goes up a notch, and I can tell he is upset.

She appears to sense this and, moving closer, whispers, "I came off the pill."

Her soft words reverberate like thunder inside the room. It's the impending storm that I have been dreading since the day Markus and I became a couple. The fault lines are broken, and next comes the fall.

"Is this deliberate? Did you plan this?" his voice echoes in the kitchen.

"Yes, but only because I didn't want to lose you. I love you, Markus."

I leave the room at this point; I'd heard enough, but I needn't have bothered as I can still hear them. I stand in the hallway outside the kitchen, shivering.

"This is not love. This is betrayal!"

"Markus, calm down," says Savannah.

I step back into the room, concerned. I have never heard him lose his cool, and I'm scared he might hurt Stacey. She is weeping uncontrollably, telling him that she is sorry, but he left her no choice; it was the only way he would stay with her. She did it to save them.

He storms out of the room, and I'm not sure what to do. Savannah comes to me and hugs me close.

"Dylan, please take him home. I'll take care of Stacey."

Her face has turned white, and her fingers tremble, so I nod and move on autopilot. I leave the room to find him, without acknowledging the inconsolable woman sitting by the fire. He's standing at the bottom of the stairs, staring at the rain. He glances up as I come down the steps. I notice Bruno relaxing in his small bed in the lounge; I'd forgotten about him.

I guess he's staying clear of the drama.

Savannah comes down to say goodbye. She hugs Markus close, and he kisses her on the forehead.

She gives me a hug, "Get home safe."

I thank her for the nice meal and for having me over. Markus is waiting at the door. He holds the umbrella open, and I go to join him. The rain is coming down in sheets, and the streetlights are barely visible. He helps me into the car.

"I can drive us home."

"It's okay, Dylan, I'll drive."

He closes the door, and I fasten my seatbelt.

Choosing Me

The Ugly Truth

I had never been in love before until now. But I recognise the signs of a broken heart. How broken? I suppose only time will tell. Markus has the same preoccupied stare that my father had for most of my childhood. The situation is not the same, but the look is identical.

When I wake up the next day, he's not in bed. Last night, I waited for him, but he did not come to me. I wonder if I should stay with him today, but I decide to go to work instead.

My stomach is tied in knots, so I can't face breakfast, but I make myself a salad for lunch. His birthday cake is in the refrigerator. I offered him a slice last night, and he did eat, but then his phone buzzed, and I went to bed.

I assumed it was her.

He cannot be angry forever. Eventually, they will have plans which won't include me.

A baby; his baby. No matter how much he says he loves me, I can never compete with that. Nor would I want to.

Her face flashes across my mind. I didn't know what she would look like, but she was lovely, even drenched in rain. Her voice was warm and sultry, her movements refined.

She is exactly the sort of woman I can easily picture him with.

The sun finally pushed through at lunchtime, and the clouds melted away, leaving a brilliant blue sky. I walk to the small park across from my office building. It was where Markus and I used to go. The grass is wet, but I spread my blanket, remove my heels, and sit. I should be hungry, but the quinoa becomes stuck in my throat, so I slowly sip from my water bottle.

"Dylan?"

I look up, shielding my eyes from the midday sun, and Toby stands watching me. He sits on my blanket, stretching out his long legs.

"I thought you had a meeting?"

"Markus called."

I nod. He looks at my uneaten salad and frowns. I start packing my lunch back into the cool bag, zipping it up.

"What did he say?"

"He told me what had happened."

I look at his lips as he speaks. His eyes are light brown in the sunlight.

"Are you alright?" he asks.

"Yes, why wouldn't I be?"

"You didn't eat your Avocado."

"You know, I somehow expected this to happen. It all felt too good to be true."

Hot tears prick the back of my eyes.

"Dylan...."

Toby put his arm around me, and I let myself cry. He smells good; he always does.

"I just wanted to have more time with him, Toby."

"You and Markus are together; this doesn't mean the end."

"Toby, she's having his baby. I could never come between a child and its parents. It would go against everything I believe in."

"D, you don't know that it's his."

"Should I stick around to find out? Then what?"

"I don't know the solution, but I think you two will work it out together. Every relationship has its problems. You don't just bail at the first sign of trouble."

"I'm scared," I admit.

"I know. Markus and I have been friends since we were fourteen, and today is the first time he has called me for help. He's scared too. He doesn't want to lose you. He loves you. We both do."

He smooths my hair away from my face; a few strands have come loose from my bun.

"Come on," he helps me up, and I dry my eyes.

He folds my blanket and packs it neatly in its bag. I pull out my compact mirror and groan. My eyes are puffy and red. I dread going back to work in this state.

Toby takes my hand as we walk out the gates of the small garden, and he hails a taxi.

"What are you doing?"

"I've signed you out so we can have the rest of the afternoon off. Borough Market?"

He helps me into the cab, and I put on my

sunglasses. He reaches for my hand as the cab does a U-turn and sets off. I lean over and kiss his cheek. He gives me a wink, and I smile. Every girl should have a Toby.

* * *

It's past midnight when I arrive home. Markus's car is parked in his usual spot, but when I enter the apartment, he is not in the lounge, and the lights are off. The room is bathed in blue from the rays of the moon. A slight breeze leads me to the balcony, and he's sitting outside with an open bottle of wine at his feet.

"Is that wise?"

He smiles when he notices me,

"Did you have a nice time?"

"I did."

He reaches his hand, gesturing for me to come to him.

"What did you do?"

I don't move an inch. I watch as his extended

hand returns to his knee.

"Went to the market and then back to Toby's. He's looking to buy a bigger place."

"Where is he looking?"

"Local. Toby loves London. He'll probably end up staying in his beloved Greenwich."

The evening is cold, so I wrap my arms around myself. Markus is wearing a light blue sweater and dark jeans. He stands, and I watch him closely to see if he will start swaying, but he appears sober. I walk further into the room as he moves towards me.

"Dylan..."

"Markus..."

We both speak at the same time.

"You go," he offers.

"What's happening with you and Stacey?"

"I haven't spoken to her."

"Why not?"

"I don't know what I can say to her."

"That you love her."

"She already knows that. She also knows that it's over between us."

"Is it?"

"Yes, it is. I'm with *you*."

"Is that why you've been shutting me out? I waited for you last night."

He exhales heavily.

"I admit I'm hurt by her actions. I didn't expect this, and I apologise for shutting you out. I was trying not to let you see."

"Is that why you called Toby?"

"Yes, I know this is upsetting for you. I got back from my run, and you had already left. I wanted to make sure you were okay."

"Did you sleep with her when you went to Paris?"

"No."

"Did you want to?"

Choosing Me

"No, it was how I knew it was finally over. The pull was gone. I no longer had any desire for her. I only want *you*."

"Over? Is it really? The way you are moping tells me something different."

"It's just we were together for a while..." he begins, but I don't need to hear this.

I can already see the pain in his eyes. Only love can hurt like that.

"What about the baby?" I whisper, breathless, even though I have not moved an inch since he walked inside.

My heart hammers against my chest, cutting off my air supply.

"I take care of my responsibilities, Dylan. I always do."

"That's comforting to know. So, I should forget that another woman is having your baby and carry on as normal?"

My voice breaks, but I persevere, wanting the

thoughts that consumed my day to be out in the open, where he can hear them.

"The situation is not ideal, but it's out of my control."

"Instead of talking to me, your first course of action is to call Toby to clean up your mess?"

"What would you like me to say?"

"What reassurance do I have? You love me, but you love *her* too. What does it mean when you love someone?"

"I do love you," he whispers softly, "Truly."

"I now have a face and a name. She's beautiful, and she blends nicely into your world. You two look perfect together."

"*You* are my world."

"Why? Tell me why you love me. What is it that makes me more special than her?"

His phone on the counter suddenly rings, startling me. I have never heard this ringer in all our time together, and I wonder if maybe he talks to her in secret. The shrill sound echoes through the room, but he does not take his eyes off me. It rings out, and I look away. He inches closer, cautiously, as if afraid that I might bolt from the room.

"Dylan, please just give me some time."

"Time to do what?"

His eyes appear conflicted. Emotions pour from behind his impenetrable mask, and I finally see what this is about. Saying goodbye in Paris was not enough. He foolishly thought it was, but his feelings are still there. Lying dormant beneath the surface, just waiting to erupt.

If he is ever to move on, then he needs to exorcise his past.

"Time to get over her? Is that what this is?" my voice comes out shrill.

He takes another step forward, and I move one backwards.

"I don't understand what is happening. But I am working through it. Fighting my way back to you," his voice breaks.

The phone rings again. I walk slowly towards it. Her name flashes across the screen, and I react. I pick it up and hurl it across the room. The impact – when it smashes into pieces – is louder than I am expecting, but he does not even flinch.

"Take all the time you need," I hiss, spinning on my heels, turning to bolt up the stairs, not wanting to be in this room one moment longer, but he reaches out his hand to grab me.

His arms are like steel, and a sliver of fear snakes down my back. He releases me, his eyes alarmed.

"I only mean to ask you to stay, *please*?"

"Stay here and watch you pine for your ex-lover?"

"Not because I want her, Dylan."

He moves his head away, tears pool in his eyes, and I instinctively wipe them away. One thing has not changed; I cannot bear to see him hurting. Before I can move my fingers away from his face, he catches them in his, bringing them to his lips.

"Then tell me why?"

"I trusted her with my life," he exhales sharply.

My resolve breaks, but, like an elephant in the room, the bigger problem still exists.

"A baby is more than love," I say.

His eyes close for the briefest of moments, and then he pulls me into his arms.

"After I'd made love to you, I would sometimes lie awake and watch you sleep for hours."

"Do you remember the day I had lunch with my mother? I walked her out to her car as she was leaving the restaurant, and you know what she said to me?"

He pauses for the briefest of moments, and I am glued to his every word, "Whatever it is that's caused this change in me, I should try to hold on to it. She knew before I did."

"You ask me why. I don't know why...but

when you smile at me, it leaves me breathless. I love that you're slightly neurotic. I love the way you always sing along to your favourite songs. I love the looks you give me when you're annoyed. I love the way you always speak your mind. I love the sound of your voice and how passionate you are about the people you love."

"I couldn't give Stacey what she wanted, and I'm sorry for that. I've always felt sorry, but with you, it's crystal clear. If she had asked me to have a child with her, I would have said no. She took that choice away from me. I'm angry and upset, but none of it compares to the thought of losing *you*. I can face anything if you are by my side."

His beautiful words linger between us; the silence is loud, stretching on and on. My heart is heavy as I know what I must do. It is the only way I can continue loving this man with everything I am.

I close my eyes, and it takes me back to another time and another place. A place that I ran away from. A motherless childhood. An empty place of longing. Four seasons viewed through a window,

Choosing Me

where every footstep that was never hers echoed in my nightmares, causing terrors so vivid, I would lie frozen for hours. The photographs of me and her together all paint the same picture. I was loved, but then it was cruelly snatched away by something that haunted me until I broke free. It was not without sacrifice.

Four years ago, my grandmother gave me a ticket to freedom. She encouraged me to leave my family behind and go seek a life where I can be happy. It is bittersweet because I can't tell her that it worked. I am here, Grams. I listened to my heart, just like you said. I found my happiness, and it brought me the man of my dreams, and for me, that is enough.

Losing the people I love is not a new concept. Not for me. I've spent my entire childhood pining for a life that was always out of my reach. My heart has already been shattered, broken into a million pieces.

I'm not afraid of that kind of pain. I've known it...for most of my life.

"The thing is, Markus, a child always needs its

parents. Not one, but two. Of course, I know that sometimes life makes it impossible for it not to be that way, but I cannot live with myself if I inflict that kind of pain. I know it well because I've lived it."

"You once told me it takes more than love for two people to stay together, and it's true. I loved the idea of us, but from the very beginning, you were never mine...I see that now."

His fingers tremble as he pulls me closer until our foreheads touch. The subtle scent of alcohol on his breath is almost intoxicating, and my head begins to spin.

"Dylan, I am yours. Let me prove it to you. Let me show you what we can be."

I move my head, but his grip on my shoulder is tight.

"I know that you love me. I love you. I'll always love you...but I can't stay here with you. Not now. Not knowing about the baby...it changes everything. Until I know for sure...I just can't."

His fingers loosen their hold on me, and my

heart rate accelerates. Cold fear grips me as the realisation of what is happening breaks like icy water over my body, drenching me until my very bones freeze over. I know what comes next, and I brace myself for it, but the only emotion my mind registers is his own. His face, always so closed off to me, is like an open book, but I avert my eyes. The pain is hard to see. All the oxygen is sucked from the room, and I turn to go, walking up the stairs while he watches me.

* * *

The red dial on the dash of the taxi reads one forty-five a.m. Markus wanted me to wait until morning, and he offered to bring me home, but I knew if I stayed the night, I would not be strong enough to leave. The driver takes a longer route to my place, and though the night is pitch black outside the window, the way is familiar to me. He came this way once. It was the day that I first realised that I never wanted to let him go.

I reach into my bag to find the cab fare.

"It's alright, love. You don't have to pay," he

says.

He must notice the puzzled look on my face.

"Picking up from that address, the tab is already prepaid. Have a good evening."

I nod, thanking him. He waits until I am inside before driving off; the taillights disappear into the night.

My apartment is cold. I remove my heels, switch on the radiators, and then turn on all the lights. Walking into my bedroom, the smell of us permeates the air. A soft subtle hint of an erotic scent that was beautiful, sexy, and sweet, but now, it is tainted with sadness.

A copy of the hobbit lies abandoned on the dresser in my spare bedroom. Some of his clothes are still in the closet. I look around at the telltale signs that remind me we were here together only a week ago, blissfully happy. I did not want to go to his penthouse in the skies. I wish we had just stayed right here. I wish he had never gone to Paris. I wish he would come to me now. I wish I knew that we were making love for the last time two days ago.

The sound of the heaters coming to life is comforting. I am still waiting for the dread and despair to hit me. I thought I would cry in the taxi on the way back to my place, but nothing happened.

I don't understand it. I love him, so why isn't my heart breaking? Why am I not screaming his name?

I grab my wash bag and head for the shower. The water is lukewarm. I slip into my old, trusted cotton pyjamas. My familiar warm bed welcomes me, and I fall into her folds and drift.

I sleep with the blinds open, and the sunlight bursts into my room, waking me up early the next day. The storage heaters have been on all night, and the apartment is boiling.

I have no plans, so I clean the apartment after showering. Fine dust has settled in my absence. Then, I dress in workout gear and head out for a run.

The local park is bustling. I try not to think about the last time Markus and I were here together.

It was that dreadful day when he told me he was going to Paris. I concentrate on my breathing technique, just like he taught me, but I am distracted by the surroundings.

Mothers and babies in brightly coloured strollers. My eyes zone in on a dad pushing a young girl on a swing, and she is squealing for him to push her higher. I soon abandon the run, sitting and observing the happy families. Reminiscing about my own childhood with Kizzy.

Everyone around us over-compensated to make us happy, but nothing could ever replace the vacant space in my heart.

As I round the bend back to my place, a sleek black Mercedes snakes out of my road, its orange light flashing to indicate it is going left, driving in the direction away from me. My heart accelerates, and I stop in my tracks. The familiar license plate — with his initial and surname — gleaming like a homing beacon, calling to me. I stand there, willing him to notice me in the rearview mirror. The dark car slows down at the amber traffic lights, but they turn green, and then…it disappears.

With dead feet, I slowly walk home, my legs like heavy weights slugging up the stairs. My fingers fumble with the keys while opening my apartment door. The door across the hall opens, and Cynthia walks out.

"Hey, Dylan. That hunk of a guy was just here looking for you."

"I went for a run."

"Is he off somewhere?"

"I don't…." my voice breaks, "Not that I know of."

"It's just that he left something in your letterbox."

"Oh. Okay, thanks," I reply, closing my door and retracing my steps back down the stairs to open my mailbox.

Cynthia follows me downstairs, chatting in her chirpy voice. She leans against the bannister and watches me as I stare at the square envelope inside, mesmerised.

"Hey, can I ask about the other guy, the bald one?" she suddenly says, breaking my trance.

"What?"

"Well, I figured now that you're with this guy. The hot one is free, right?"

"Toby and I are just friends."

My voice sounds strange to my ears, but my eyes never leave the envelope. I want Cynthia to go away, but I don't want to be rude. I did ask her to keep an eye on my place while I was gone, but I didn't know I would be back home so soon.

"How about we all go out for drinks sometime? Have you ever been to the magic mushroom? It's just out past the underground bunker...."

"Cynthia. Sorry, Toby already has someone else."

"Oh. That's a shame," she says.

I turn to go running up the stairs without a

backward glance. The envelope feels like it weighs a ton. My fingers tremble: it smells like warm apples. I walk slowly to my lounge and sit, pulling the flap open. Inside is a note written in his hand.

Hot tears sting my eyes as the floodgates finally break, cutting off my air supply. The hollow dread begins to spread through my body, and I close my eyes to absorb the impact.

I've been here before,

I repeat this in my head, over and over, but as the seconds slowly tick by, every breath slices like a knife tearing through my lungs, and I cannot breathe.

This does not feel the same. It's not like before.

My heart was breaking then, but now, it feels like my blood is draining out of me, replaced by coldness.

"Markus!"

I scream his name, but no sound will come, so when his voice calls out to me, a burst of heat shoots through my entire body. I run to the door, yanking it open.

Toby, handsome and steadfast, stands on the other side. He steps inside and pulls me into his arms. They are not the arms I crave, but they are enough for now. My tears stain his shirt, and he lifts me up, takes me to the lounge, and sits on the couch, cradling me in his lap, the thick silky paper still clutched tight in my grasp.

Choosing Me

Dylan,

Sometimes life gives you a gift,
In the moments when you least expect it.
You find a rose amongst the thorns,
And suddenly, the dark days are forever gone.
Goodbye does not always mean the end,
For happiness may be just around the bend.

These past few months have been the best of my life.
Thank you for choosing me.
- M

A note about the author

D S Johnson - Mills hails from the tiny tropical Island of Montserrat, B.W.I. Her father is a songwriter and was the reigning calypso monarch for much of her childhood.

Her favourite subject at school was English, so writing comes to her naturally.

She created the main male character for her novel after being inspired by someone she once met. He had a piercing stare, and she was mesmerised, trying to figure out his thoughts. He was quite attractive in an understated way, so she devised her own version of events.

When she started writing about this perfect stranger, she struggled to create the essence of him. Hence, she decided to introduce her female protagonist.

The only thing missing was how they would meet. That's when her third character came into the picture and refused to go away.

She currently resides in England with her husband and son and perseveres to write every single day.

This is her debut novel, and many more are yet to come.

Printed in Great Britain
by Amazon